Joey Roembke Heart and Soul

Joey Roembke Heart and Soul

Raymond Joseph Roembke

Raymond Joseph Roembke
2014

First Printing: 2014

Raymond Joseph Roembke
2960 Locust Circle
Indianapolis, Indiana 46227
www.barbclaire@sbcglobal.net

ISBN: 978-1-312-34235-4

Dedication

To my family and many teachers who have inspired and shared with me their love for learning.

Thank you. Without your support and patience, I would have never achieved my dream.

Contents

Acknowledgements

I would like to thank my family and many teachers without whose help this book would never have been completed. Thank you for your patience and guidance; you were unfailing in your willingness to provide last minute reviews and editing of my many projects the last four years.

Thank you to Betsy Mader who provided all of the photography in this book. (www.betsymaderphotography.com)

Thank you to Aunt Barb for many hours reviewing each and every page of this book to make sure it was the best it could be.

A special thank you to all who have provided me feedback about my writing, especially Mrs. Anderson who has helped me find my own voice through writing. I appreciate her willingly sharing her thoughts and allowing me to include it in the Forward of my book.

I have had so many extraordinary teachers. There is one teacher, however, who continues to influence me. Mrs. Jordan took a student who struggled with reading and encouraged me to read to her kindergarten class. The kids didn't judge me or give me a letter grade, didn't notice when I skipped or changed words, and were enthused to hear me read. It changed my outlook on reading and school in general. I will always be grateful. Thank you so much.

Foreword

Student writing often suffers from voice, experience, style. From the moment Joey sat down at a table to write, I knew he already came with the "right stuff." His unique story and viewpoint infused his personal narratives, creative nonfiction, and short stories, showing maturity, sensitivity and perspective. Since that time a few years ago, Joey has presented me with the gift of reading his new works, allowing me to offer insights, constructive criticism, and plaudits as he grows into a polished writer. Teachers and mentors yearn for a student such as Joey, one who understands the importance of learning and education. I consider my life enriched having enjoyed this opportunity to participate in Joey's formative writing years.

Cheri Anderson
Creative Writing Instructor
April, 2014.

Preface

It has been a dream of mine to publish a book since my freshman year in high school. Writing allows me to have a unique voice and to share my point of view. In grade school, my struggles with dyslexia made it difficult to put my thoughts on paper. In high school, I began to write as a way to deal with a difficult situation. The more I wrote the more I liked it. It was healing to put those words on paper. My teachers encouraged me to write and develop my own style. This book represents my work in the last four years. It is my hope that as you read *Joey Roembke Heart and Soul* you will enjoy it as much as I enjoyed writing each and every word of it.

Section 1: Reflections and Poetry

The Power of Hands

Our hands tell who we are. They are believed to be perfect subjects of the mind. As physical labor shows in the calluses on our palms, so does gentleness or greediness or strength. Nothing else expresses human behavior in so many ways. With our hands, we work, play, love, threaten, show joy or grief. Sensitive symbols of faith and friendship, our hands draw to us everything and everyone we love. Marvelously made and directed by the mind's eye, the mind's ear, and the heart's desire, our hands continually express our lives. An abusive hand is from an abusive mind. But the gentle touch does exist – even for those who have yet to experience it. What words cannot say, the hand can express with all tenderness and love. Our hands do many great things for us that we tend to take for granted. Our hands show how we feel without speaking a word; our hands help us teach, and they help us direct people. My grandma could not speak when her tumor began to take over her brain. My grandpa laid his hands on top of hers to show he would be there until the end and that he loved her more than anything, even in her darkest hour. He did not say it; he used his hands to show it. Our hands are powerful tools we use to pray, but we cannot pray unless our hands come together. Remember to take time to bring your hands together and pray.

So today I ask of you to get to know your hands better. Observe them in action and at rest. Notice all the tasks they perform for you today.

God, Giver of All Gifts, I thank you for my hands-which I often take for granted until I have an injury or arthritis. I thank you for all the marvelous things I can do with my hands. I know when Jesus came to earth he used his hands well to heal the sick, to feed the hungry, to play with children, to console the grieving, to pray, to break bread of the Eucharist, and finally to receive the nails on the cross out of love for us. Loving God, help me to use my hands well as Jesus did to serve others in your name.
Amen

Thankful

I am thankful for my relationship with God because without it I know I would be nothing. I am thankful for my family; they give me support and build me up when I am down. I am thankful for my teachers who give up their time and effort to teach me and help me become successful. I am thankful for my mom who raised me, cares and loves me and shows me love every day. I am thankful for my friends because they treat me like I am family and make me feel comfortable. I am thankful for the obstacles God gives me and the lessons he teaches me. Thank you for everything in my life Lord.

Amen.

Where I'm From

I am from a family
from members whose love is as big as the universe

I am from grass and dirt
from home plate, white lines and people in face masks

I am from lines on a court
from a ten foot basket and an orange ball

I am from numbers like math
from sand and one hundred meters

I am from green grass
from clubs, carts, and caddies

I am from a school where there is no color
from a principal who only sees white and not black

I am from a neighborhood
from friends with works bombs, bonfires, and fireworks

I am from Hocus Pocus Joey on Locust
performing tricks like an acrobat

I am from sounds sweet as ripe berries
from keyboards, strings, and brass

I am from Destiny's Step Child
from playing bass to the sounds of rock and blues

I am from a church
from Catholic teaching

I am from St. Roch CYO a tether to my roots
from laser tag, putt putt, and service projects

I am from the Wizard's guard
from Dorothy, scarecrow, lion, tin man, and Toto

My Gifts

What gifts I bring you ask
Now I look upon my past

Once an athlete thought I
Whether basketball, golf, or track, I run, I fly

I wondered is it music I bring
The sounds from instruments I love but do not sing

Is it friendships I share
On Twitter, Facebook, and everywhere

Is it family, we're so close
They support me the most

I now know it isn't any of these
But an opportunity I must seize

It is diversity I brought has had the most impact
Shedding the light on education we lack

A different person once broken hearted
Changed forever from when I started

Now stronger, wiser, put to the test
To stand up for others I'll do my best

Cause who I am matters ya know
Afro-American Sophomore Joe

Equality

"So even though we face the difficulties
of today and tomorrow, I still have a dream.
It is a dream deeply rooted
in the American dream.
I have a dream that one day this nation
will rise up and live out
the true meaning of its creed:
We hold these truths to be self-evident
that all men are created equal.
I have a dream…" Martin Luther King Jr.

Words from a great man who wanted equal rights
For all people no matter if they were black or white
MLK had a dream
Peacefully he took it mainstream

Inspiring peace while fighting the fight
Martin Luther King fought for Civil Rights
A life too short was taken
A bullet ended his life but his message could not be shaken

MLK was a light that shown for all to see
He saw what life could be
His message like waves coming to shore
Crashed and spread on the sand

Peaceful, powerful, person who persevered
Never letting go of his dream
He was a rock
A foundation for equality today

Inspiring us young and old
He was like a father to us all
His message was sure and strong
His love of all was undeniable

I am better because I have heard his message
I am different because it touched my heart
I also have a dream
That one day we can all not see in black and white

Music

Life plays us like music
she plays it right
we sing a nice lyric
she plays it wrong
we sing a sad song
some goes to the top
some never stop,
getting dropped
BUT LIFE IS
LIKE MUSIC
hip hop, rock,
pop and reggae
we put it together
we get a song on
a Sunday
BUT LIFE IS
LIKE MUSIC
many play it
so nice
you know they
are hitting the charts
better be careful
people
before it drives
you nuts
some pop till
they drop
they never get
back up
next thing you know
they're selling rocks
to climb back to the top
BUT LIFE IS LIKE MUSIC
so if you know it's got a nice tone
sing it and never look back
cause life gives you one sheet
make music and make
everyone clap

Places Life Takes Us

Mountain
High rocky
Running, looking, hiking
Eagle, power, fear, rabbit
Living, moving, making noise
Deep, beautiful
Ocean

Football
Cool, tough
Tiring, passing, playing
Helmet, shoulder pads, club cart
Putting, concentrating, driving
Smooth swing
Golf

Night
Bitter, dark
Sleeping, snoring, dreaming
Solitary, lonely, cheerful, bright
Playing, running, smiling
Sunny, warm
Day

Dreams
Subconscious, imaginary
Sleeping, wishing, thinking
Fantasy, actuality, vision, genuine
Being, seeing, knowing, authentic, factual
Reality

Fire
Hot, bright
Burning, flaming, glaring
Blazing, raging, tranquil, solid
Chilling, freezing, cooling
Frigid, frosty
Ice

The Beauty of Simplicity

Jack
a man
went up a hill
dummy

Tiger
athlete
cheated on wife
golfer

A knock
people approach
to see who is there
everything stops and man reached
door opens

The Poetry of Nature

Green grass in April
Birds begin to sing in trees
Children playing outside

In spring flowers bloom
In spring animals come out
Best of all...it's warm

Waves upon the sand
Ice melts as spring approaches
Warmer weather soon

Butterflies hatch
Bees drink the juice from flowers
Bees fly everywhere

Snow falling slowly
Blanketing the trees and road
Silence and beauty

Fall is leaves falling,
Munching on sweet red apples
A warm fire burning

As the wind does blow
Across the trees, I see the
Buds blooming in May

Lesson from the Past

The end of the week finally arrived. I told my wife I was going to my childhood town right after work, and I wouldn't arrive home until late into the night. I couldn't wait to stop at my favorite boyhood café, Johnny's. I finished up the last papers that were stacked on my desk, put them in the desk drawer, and locked up my office. I told my secretary, Abbey, I was leaving and that the paperwork was in my desk. She said, "Sounds good Mr. Roembke. Have a wonderful weekend." "You do the same, Abbey", I replied while heading out the door.

The trip to my boyhood home was about a hundred miles, which takes around two hours to get there depending on traffic. Knox is a small town out in the country. What I liked most about growing up in Knox was the lack of noise at night. There was no noise from cars honking or the screeching of rubber tires; it was peaceful and quiet.

The weather outside was humid and sticky. I put the top down on my 1997 Ford Mustang and enjoyed the light breeze coming in from the North. My Mustang started making an unfamiliar noise. The radiator started to get loud, steam was pouring out from under the hood like a chimney in the winter, and soon she came to a complete stop. I was only a few feet away from the gas station and car repair shop.

I walked the couple of steps to the repair shop and knocked on the garage door. I knocked once more and called out, "Hello? Is there anyone here? Hello?" The garage door creaked as it arose slowly and out of the darkness appeared a tall, lanky man. The man stood about six feet five inches; his pin-striped mechanic suit was stained black, his hands were rough and cut up, and the smell of oil filled the air. He was a typical knee-jerk. I thought, "Hello sir; my Mustang broke down, and I was hoping you could take a look at her for me". The man pulled a cherry red rag from the pocket of his suit, scratched his head, and said, "I can take a look at her sir, but I can't promise I will be able to fix her. The name is Jack by the way". "I'm Ray. Just do what you can Jack. I might just have to let her go" I said. Jack chuckled and said, "You just might, but I will see what I can do for you. Let's go push her up here and see what we have to work with". Jack and I walked down the road and pushed the car up to the garage area.

I popped the hood on the car for Jack, and steam came rushing out. Jack had a distraught look on his face. "What's wrong with her Jack?" I asked eagerly. Jack replied, "Your radiator overheated number one, uh… number two your engine needs a tune-up, and number three your oil needs to be changed." I put my face in my hands feeling hopeless. Jack closed the hood and came over to me and said, "Don't worry stranger I can fix her for you, but it will take a couple days. Is that okay?" "Yes sir it is. I'm going into town to visit my boyhood home and spend a couple days anyway" I said. Jack said, "Perfect, I will have her done in a day or so." I told Jack thanks for his help and started the short walk to town.

The blistering temperature was taking a toll on me. I loosened my bowtie, unlaced my saddle oxfords, and unbuttoned a few buttons on my shirt trying to cool myself down. I continued to walk for a short period of time, but the heat was just too much for me. My body started to break down, sweat was running profusely down my face, and my knees started to shake and become weak. My body could not take much more of this heat. Everything started spinning around me, my vision was becoming blurred, and I collapsed on the jagged and searing road.

I don't know how long that ray of sunlight had been peeking through the gap in the curtains before it found its way to my face; nor do I know how long it took me to become aware of it. I didn't know what happened or where I was for that matter. I could smell something cooking and could hear people talking in the room next to me. I pulled the cover back and went to find someone who could tell me where I was and what in the world happened to me. I walked into the room where I heard people talking. I poked my head around and a man said, "Good morning stranger. How are you feeling?" "Where am I? What happened to me?" I replied. The man said to me, "Well sir, I was on my way back from work and noticed you had passed out from the dreaded heat of the day. You were lying in the middle of the road, so I picked you up and brought you to my home". I said, "Thank you that was kind of you to do for me. I'm Ray by the way. I just dropped off my Mustang at Jack's down the street and was coming down here to visit my boyhood home." The man was wearing a black suit jacket with a plain white tee shirt underneath; he had on linen pants and wore black loafers. The man looked like he was trying to pull off the Miami Vice look from the 80's. He replied, "Well I see, take a seat Ray. My name is Martin and this is my wife Lisa." The woman was wearing a vivid-colored jacket with a silk blouse underneath, the jacket looked bigger where her shoulders were, and her hair was down and curled at the ends. The man and woman both looked like they were from a different era. I didn't think much of it because this must have been side-affects from the fall I had.

I said, "Nice to meet you both and thank you again for bringing me into your home." "It's not a problem Ray. I was glad to help." Martin replied. I had breakfast and read the paper with Martin for a while. I noticed the paper was dated wrong and the headlines read "Ronald Reagan Wins Election". I thought I was imagining things again because of my fall. I said to Martin, "Thank you very much for picking me up and bringing me into your home and for breakfast." "I was glad to help out Ray. You're welcome. I will see you around" Martin replied. I grabbed my jacket off the coat rack, slipped on my shoes, and headed into town.

The town was just as I had remembered it. The old clothing stores were still around, the same bars my father used to go to were still there, and all the houses and buildings looked like they were still from the 80's. Maybe they were just trying to keep the beauty of the town; I thought to myself or maybe I somehow have time traveled back to when I was a child. Time travel has not even been discovered yet; I must be going crazy or something. I walked to the park where I used to play when I was a kid to see if it had changed. I used to go to the park with my dad after dinner every evening and throw the baseball and ride the merry-go-round. My dad told me to carve my name into a tree, so when I had kids of my own someday I could show them where I grew up. Unfortunately, the tree was cut down a couple years later because it was old and started to decay.

I arrived at the park entrance and walked to where the tree had been to see if somehow it was still there. The tree used to be behind an old wooden green bench that looked out over the White River. I walked on a narrow dirt road that followed the river and would lead me straight to the tree. I could see the green bench and to my surprise there was a tree behind it. I thought once more to myself that there is no way this is the tree I carved my name into many years ago. I walked around the tree and saw the letters "RJR" carved into the tree with the number three below it. There it was right before my eyes my initials and my baseball number, carved into the same spot in the same tree from many years ago. I removed my glasses from my face, rubbed my eyes, looked at the carving again, rubbed my eyes once more, shook my head and looked at the carving again, and it was still there; I wasn't seeing things.

I sat down on the green bench and watched the sun sink down over the river. The sky was pink and orange, the sun was a dazzling orange as well, and the river was like a mirror reflecting the sun's image down upon it. It was a gorgeous sight and watching the sunset was the only way I could keep my mind off the carving in the tree. As I lay back on the bench, my eyes became sleepy, and I fell into a deep slumber.

The sun crept up over the river, and the rays shined onto my face. I stretched out my arms and legs, cracked my back, and held my stomach as it growled loudly. I checked my watch; it was only 6:30 a.m. but to me it felt like it was noon or so. I wanted to go to Johnny's to see how much it changed or if it had changed at all. Johnny's was about three or four miles from the park. I always enjoyed the walk as a kid, especially at this time of the year. The weather usually was cooler, humidity was low, and the sky was cloudless. I began my lengthy walk to Johnny's.

As I was walking down the path, I noticed a young boy and his father throwing a baseball back and forth. The baseball gloves they were wearing were older models. The gloves were rough, brown leather, with five cut out fingers and no web stitching; the pocket area over the palm had a strap. The glove was shaped exactly like a human hand, which was odd because they don't make them like that anymore. Things were becoming more and more strange as the day passed by. I walked over and sat down on a bench to get a closer look at the man and his son.

The older man looked like my father, and the boy looked like me when I was a young boy. The man stood about six feet one inch, his hair was as black as the night sky and curled to perfection, and his face was craggy with a rough 5 o'clock shadow. He was bullnecked and healthy and well-dressed from head to toe. The suit the man had on was cut to precision, bold across the shoulders, gentle lines around the waist, the perfect inverted triangle: black, satin lapels, just the right length, and subtle movement. The man had to be my father; everything was alike. The build, the facial features, and the fashion were all there. I always carried a picture of my father and me in my wallet. I pulled the picture out and held it up to compare. The picture was like a mirror image of the man. The man was my father. The young boy with my father had to be me because I was an only child. The only way to figure this out was to follow my father back to his house to see if it was my boyhood home. If they went back to the house, then my crazy theory that somehow I was blasted back to the past would be true. I didn't want to believe this, but facts are facts, and I had to face the music.

My father called out, "Raymond come on it is almost time for dinner, and mother doesn't like us to be late." The younger version of me replied, "Coming pop". I waited awhile before I started following them. I kept my distance, but kept them in sight. They entered into a neighborhood called "Perry Manor"; the same neighborhood where I lived as a kid. They turned onto a street called "Amber Way" the same street I lived on. They proceeded a block or so further, then turned and walked up to their house.

The house was just like I remembered. The old wooden stairs led to the screened-in porch, with the swinging chair hanging from the ceiling and the old rusty door that creaked after opening and closing it. This was it; this was my boyhood home. I couldn't fathom it. I don't know how or why I was blasted back in time. I had to get to the bottom of it; however, I only had a couple hours left before I had to go pick up my car from Jack's repair shop.

I saw little Raymond playing football in the front yard. The ball came over where I was sitting. I grabbed it for him and little Raymond called out, "Hey stranger you look like me". I said, "I am you, just twenty years from now." Little Raymond had a frightened look on his face and quickly darted into the street. A car hit little Raymond. My leg was in excruciating pain. I realized whatever happened to little Raymond affected me as well.

The man driving the car quickly went to go get my father. My father called 911, and they rushed little Raymond to the hospital. My father came over to me and asked, "Do you know what happened here sir?" I looked at him and said, "Yes sir I do. I told your son Raymond that I was him twenty years from now. He was startled by this and darted into the street. A car came and hit him injuring his leg."

I pulled out an old picture of my father and me when I was a kid. My father looked at it, then looked at me, then looked at the photo again. Then he said, "You're my son from the future. What are you doing here?"

I replied, "I don't know; I was somehow transported back into the past."

He sat me down on the bench and said, "Listen son, everyone has their time, and instead of looking behind you, you should look ahead because the happiness you are seeking may be in the places you haven't looked yet. My father went back inside, got his keys and left for the hospital.

I thought about what my father said and headed back up to Jack's auto repair.

I arrived at Jack's and asked him, "What year is it?"

Jack chuckled and said, "2012 Ray. Did you have a fall or something; you're walking with a limp?"

I looked down at my leg and noticed something was wrong. I said to Jack, "Yeah, is the car ready yet?"

"She is; here are the keys" Jack said.

I drove off and headed back home. I realized I needed to let the past go and live my life as it is and that will bring me the happiness I have been looking for. The past was like an anchor weighing me down, and my father reminded me of this. I am finally going to cut the rope and let go of the past to make room for my future.

Float Away

It's 10:30 p.m. and I smell smoke. Instead of jumping out of bed and yelling "fire!" like most fifth graders would have, I snuggle deeper into my pillow with a smile. I can feel the thrum of the bass like a slow pulse coursing through the floor beneath my bed. The dark, warm air around me vibrates each time the drumstick strikes the trap, quivering just above the cool raspy slide of the steel brush caressing the snare. A saxophone lowly moans. Its melody creeps around the edges of my door, hovering along with the cigarette smoke like a cloud across the moonbeams coming in through my window. In my mind, I can trace the smoke back to the cigarette clinging unsteadily to my dad's lip as he hunches over the keyboard. At least an inch of ash hangs forgotten over his fingers as his fingers spider dance over the keys. I can hear his harmonies and intricate turns weaving under and over and around the melody.

Over the years, this experience was repeated often. Sometimes it was just my dad I heard practicing riffs and scales, melodies and harmonies. Other times the basement or garage was filled with my dad's friends jamming together. My dad's band only played jazz music. They played at many different clubs, bars, and other events every weekend. I did not see my dad much during the week with studying, homework, sports and other things popping up. Every Sunday he would come home late and always have a story to tell me about his trip. This was the only time we could catch up with each other.

My dad always carried around a giant book that contained all of his band's songs, chords, lyrics, and notes. He let me look through the book sometimes. When I get older I want to do the same thing my dad does. My dad always told me to practice every day; every day set a goal, and achieve it each day while I was practicing. I started playing the songs in his book every night. I played the songs on guitar, piano and saxophone. I did not know which instrument I wanted to play for the rest of my life so I picked up my three favorite. My dad was very pleased with me. I was moving through the songs quickly and acing every note.

One night I was practicing like normal and stumbled upon a song that had an X through it. I could still make out the notes and the lyrics. I did not know why my dad crossed this song out; the lyrics were precise, catchy, and up-tempo. I started playing the song on the saxophone because that was the first instrument indicated on the music sheet. I put the reed up to mouth, positioned my fingers on the first note which was B flat and blew a big breath out. The note echoed throughout the whole house and my dad suddenly busted through the door and yelled, "What are you doing?" I said, "What? Dad I am just playing the song." "Do not play that song son; did you not see the X through it?" my dad responded. I asked why and received no answer back. My dad turned out the light and said, "Goodnight I love you and will tell you in the morning." "I love you too dad," I said. I crawled into my warm bed, pulled the covers over my head and proceeded to sleep.

The sun crept through the trees and found itself shining bright in my window. Morning was finally here I thought to myself, time for dad to tell me the story. I quickly jumped out of bed and ran down the stairs. There was breakfast on the table; the smell of perfectly cooked bacon tickled my nostrils. I sat down and started to dig in. I dropped my fork and noticed there was a note sitting on the chair next to me. The note read, "Dear Joe, I have gone to the store for some supplies. I will be back in an hour. Love, Dad." I shrugged my shoulders and thought to myself this was a lame excuse my dad put together to avoid telling me this story. Maybe he did have to go to the store, but I highly doubted it.

I finished my complaining and eating breakfast. I went to the couch, sat down, grabbed the remote, and turned on some cartoons. Saturday morning cartoons always kept my mind off things so hopefully it could work its magic today. I turned to my favorite show Tom and Jerry, kicked my feet up and relaxed. I finally heard the garage door open; I felt like I waited an eternity. I rolled out of the chair and raced to the door. To my surprise, my mom walked through. My mom said, "Hey honey who were you looking for?" I told her I was looking for dad to come home because he owed me a story. My mom said, "I don't know when he will be home; I'm sorry honey." "It's ok mom," I said. I went back to the chair and turned the television back on. I tried to relax but this story thing was lingering in my head. I was going to go crazy if my dad did not get here soon.

Hours passed and my dad finally stepped through the door. He came in and started to tell the story. He told me back in the day when he first started the band the song with the X was the first song they wrote and played. They were playing at an outdoor stage in Las Vegas Nevada one night and picked that song to open with. The stage was in a neighborhood with tall buildings boxing it in. The sax player began, followed by the drummer then the guitar and finally the singer began to sing. Everything was going smoothly until all of a sudden all the men in the audience started to float away. The song title was "Float Away." My dad said his band stopped playing and the men came down. They played the song again in Ireland and the same thing happened, the men started floating up to the sky.

I was in disbelief at first and said, "This is a bunch of malarkey, dad!" My dad threw me my sax, put the song in front of me, and said "Play it." I began to play the first note, and then my dad followed. I walked outside playing the song to see if this really would happen. I looked up to the sky in disbelief. There, before me, were men floating in the sky. I removed my mouth from the sax and the men floated back down from where they came. My dad just looked at me and smiled. He put his arm around me and said, "Son, the power of music is unbelievable and can lead to crazy things. Never underestimate the power music holds." I said, "I won't dad. I promise." My dad walked back inside and I sat on the curb thinking. I thought maybe my dad is right maybe music does hold some sort of power. The world may never know what true power music holds or about the song that made men randomly float in the air. I guess I will just have to ask the big man upstairs when I get there.

Perfection

The days of summer linger in the moist breeze of fall that gently sweeps through a ballpark made from cement dreams of winning a World Series. The ballpark of 35,000 is filled with the chant, "Perfect." It's early in the break of the wildcard race and a crucial period in professional baseball. For the surfacing hero of this afternoon's pastime, it is a moment to see life through a different focus. It is a moment when a harmonious pulse dictates the thought, which in turn initiates a perfect action in a particular frame in time, or what athletes call the zone. Bryan Thacker is a hero who, though young, is infinitely defined by the heroes of a time long before him. In the announcer's booth high above home plate, the voices of hometown color commentator's Ray Roembke and Jerry Cummings invade the ballpark accompanying the excitement, which is felt by the chant echoing throughout the stands.

"Ladies and gentlemen welcome back to the game! I'm Ray Roembke along with my partner Jerry Cummings. We are witnessing an amazing display of athletic excellence today by a young man named Bryan Thacker! Thacker has been perfect for eight and 2/3 innings of work so far and will attempt to close this game out by retiring one more batter in the top half of the ninth; The Reds lead the game one to nothing! You have to ask yourself, what a pitcher must be thinking, when in a crucial situation like this, don't you think so Jerry?" "You sure do Ray! In a situation like this I am almost certain that Thacker isn't worried about anything else but getting one more out! The one out that will capitalize on this valiant effort, which could very easily become part of baseball history.

The home plate umpire throws Thacker a fresh white baseball. As Thacker catches the baseball, he is met with a roar of cheers from the fans who rise to their feet and with out-stretched arms repeatedly bow down in praise of their ace pitcher. Thacker wipes the sweat from his face, grips his metal spikes on the rubber and stretches out to receive the sign from the catcher. A flood of boos fills the stands as the stadium loudspeakers announce the third batter of the ninth inning. The announcer lowly mumbles the player's name in a monotone growl, but with great decibel control to clearly pronounce the player's name, so that the fans are certain of their directed hatred, "Now, up for the visiting Saint Louis Cardinals, first baseman Jack Madden!"

The crowd is instantly driven into a violent frenzy full of verbal attacks as the fans spot the man who could instantly shatter their dreams. Madden is a monstrous opponent who would dwarf any man's courage. He stands a grand six feet, ten inches tall. His body, shaped in cone fashion with silver-colored plastic body armor covering every patch of flesh, is broken up only by his black jersey. The true identity of the all-star slugger is further disguised with a beard. A piece of armor is sewn to his jersey, which resembled a mask robbers wore in the Old West. It was a black shadow that hid his face from the very fans that were responsible for his success in the game of baseball no more than a year ago. Madden, a former Red, was a major contributor in last season's miracle division clinching club that was prematurely eliminated in the first round of the playoffs at the hands of the Saint Louis Cardinals.

The crowd begins to chant, "Traitor", as Madden walks to the batter's box, where he stops mid-stride and tips his batter's helmet to the crowd. The fans, instigated by Madden's actions, begin to shout profanity and wave obscene gestures at the all-star slugger who is working for the cycle on the afternoon. The relentless crowd continues to harass Madden with the chant of "overrated", until in response he points his bat to the center field stands where the bleacher bums hold up handmade signs that read "On the eighth day God sent us Thacker."

Thacker is on the mound sixty feet away from the greatest challenge in his career. He grinds his spikes into the front ground of the pitcher's mound and wipes his forehead in harmony with every second grind he makes in the sand. The crowd once again rises to their feet and begins to chant "perfect" to support their hero in what they realize is the most pivotal moment of the game. Thacker looks into the crowd and tips his cap in appreciation, only to be cut short by a tremor that overcomes his right hand. The nerves begin to eat at Thacker as he continues to wipe sweat from his forehead and grind the mound with his spikes, occasionally rubbing his hands over the baseball. He'd never really noticed until now how warm it gets when the sun begins to set and it beams down on the pitcher's mound. Apparently some genius decided to face the ballpark toward the west when obviously the sun would blind the pitcher in any afternoon game, Thacker thought. The mound began to feel as if it was centered by a spotlight that has turned on its high beam to blind and dehydrate Thacker who continues to sweat profusely.

As Madden approaches the plate, catcher Chris Fey holds up a hand toward the home plate umpire and signals for a timeout, so that he may conference with his hurler. "Timeout!" shouts the masked official. Fey trots to the mound, greeting Thacker with a grin that seems to connect his ears. "Pretty exciting game, hey Bryan" Fey says while taking the baseball from Thacker's glove and placing it into his. "How are you feeling?" "Other than feeling like a hot tamale, I'm fine," Thacker responds in a voice laboring to find oxygen to speak. "That sun is roasting my ass, man." "I should get an assist in this game you know," Fey says. "What are you talking about?" Thacker asks while rearranging his cap, which is soaked with sweat. "Hell, Bryan, along with your high heater, my stomach has given you an edge over these boys," Fey says, as he rubs his stomach underneath his chest protector. "You didn't see Tyler Morgan's jerk back last inning when you threw that slider inside?" "I saw a weird look on his face, but I really didn't think about it much," Thacker replied. "Well, when the pitch was about five feet from the plate, my stomach let out a God-awful groan that made him turn his head. The umpire barely got out the words strike three." Thacker looks back over to home plate and sees the umpire refer to the time by pointing to his watch. Fey turns back to his friend, who now looks more focused on the game. "Are you feeling better now Bryan?" "Yeah, I was getting kind of tense, but now I'm better," Thacker says while he wipes his blood shot eyes stinging with sweat. "Then let's get back to business!" Fey snaps. "You know this guy, and you know what he can do, so take it nice and easy and remember keep your pitches away from the inside half! If you get nervous, just think about that night we had in Chicago and how we're going to party down tonight once you get this last out! I know you can do it, so let's hand this guy some bench and go eat!"

Fey with an arrogant smile hands Thacker the ball and runs back to home plate holding two fingers in the air toward the fielders signaling the out count. Thacker continues his pre-pitch routine warm-up and digs a deeper divot into the mound, while searching past thoughts for some piece of mind that will help him shake the nervousness.

Thacker begins mumbling a piece of advice his father gave him when he was five years old. "If it gets tough out there, either get nasty or go home." Easy for him to say, he thought, as he dwelled on his father's baseball career. Thacker snaps out of his thoughts and tries to calm down and focus on Madden, who has 35 homeruns on the season and is batting .312 going into the end of the season. Thacker again begins to drift off and think about everything that could go wrong and how he can drop from number one to nothing in a snap. Thacker's thoughts are once again broken as the home plate umpire barks for the game to resume by shouting "play ball".

Thacker leans forward on his left knee, squints his eyes in an attempt to block the sun, as he examines the signal that Fey flashes rapidly between his legs. He wipes his eyes and tries to remember what 2-3-1-right-1 means. Slider high and outside, maybe, Thacker thinks. "Here comes Thacker's' first pitch!" Jerry shouts. "Outside corner strike one! It was a picture perfect slider high on the outside corner!" The crowd erupts into cheers and begins chanting "perfect" as they start to bow down in praise once more. Thacker shakes his head in disbelief, wondering why Madden had laid off of a pitch that would make any hitter in the league salivate with homerun hunger. The feeling fades, though, as he begins grinding into the pitcher's mound again hoping that he can stay ahead on the count against a hitter who doesn't repeat mistakes often. Ahead on the count, kind of like he was with the women in Chicago. "Chicago, God that night was one of those half good, half bad times," he mumbles to himself.

Thacker shakes off a sign that he can hardly see. Fey flashes the same sign again trying to get Thacker's focus back on the game. Thacker shakes him off again, leaving Fey no other choice, than to flash the go ahead sign. Fey flips his catcher's mitt open and prepares for the unknown, hoping the pitch will be out of Madden's reach. "Thacker is playing it safe Ray," Jerry comments, as he watches Thacker lean forward on his knee preparing for his windup. "He is taking his time and keeping Madden off balance! It is a show of great poise, considering the pressures of pitching in such a tense situation!" Thacker initiates his delivery and leans back, balancing on his right leg, finally barreling forward, releasing a lightening thrust of a pitch heading straight for Madden's chest. The ball breaks just under Madden's jerked-back arms as the umpire calls ball one. "Wow that pitch almost got away from Thacker! It was a bit odd to throw some chin music right there?" Ray questions. "Kind of risky on Thacker's part, try really risky on Thacker'" Jerry shouts. "If Madden hadn't lifted his arms, the perfect game would have ended with a hit batter and an automatic walk! Thacker must be feeling the effects of throwing over 105 pitches!"

Fey throws Thacker the baseball while motioning downward with his glove to tell him to settle down. He sees the sign and snatches the baseball from the air, nodding his head in disgust. He goes to the back of the mound and grabs the talcum powder bag to dry his hands, but the anger inside of him prevents him from grabbing it firmly, causing the bag to slip from his grasp. He pulls his cap off and rubs his arm sleeve across his forehead to soak up some of the sweat dripping into his eyes. The sun's setting rays shine brilliantly, illuminating the mound fully, and gleaming sweat off of Thacker's exposed forearms and face. He leans forward and pulls the rim of his cap down, allowing him to see a blurred shadow of the signal Fey flashes, a 4-2-right-1-1. It's a cut fastball, Thacker thinks, as he enters his wind-up to deliver some inside heat.

Madden swings at the pitch sending an ear-piercing crack throughout the stadium. A vacuum of silence takes the air out of the stands for a moment, finally breaking into a gasp of cheers as the baseball floats into foul territory. Thacker stares into the clouds and gives a quick reference to God by pointing into the sky. The tremors now consume his entire body, causing him to bend over on his left knee, with his head sagging down toward the sand on the pitcher's mound.

Thacker tries to gather himself and glares toward home plate trying to see what Fey signals. He flashes 3-2-1-right-2. High heat over the outside half of the plate, Thacker thinks to himself. The sun suddenly shifts and dives halfway below the home plate stands, splitting its rays down the foul lines. Thacker looks around and shakes his head to clear the images of spotted colors from his blurred sight, when he sees her in the stands surrounded by a heavenly glow. There in the second row behind the home team dugout immersed in a flood of the sun's setting rays, he sees the reason for his success and recent pain. He sees his wife standing, holding her hands to her heart and staring into his eyes, watching his every movement. A weight is lifted from his mind as he reads his wife's lips that say, "I know you can do it."

Thacker reaches up and tips his cap in her direction without a single tremor. He then turns back toward home plate and with a smile stares into Madden's eyes that are as lifeless as sharks' eyes when it attacks its prey. Thacker glances at the sign Fey flashes for the second time, but this time he nods his head in acceptance. He lifts himself up in his stance and begins his delivery by pulling his body back, balancing on his right leg and thrusting forward hurling a fastball that blurs into a white streak, nicks the top of Madden's bat. The ball floats high into the air and seems to hover over the pitcher's mound for an eternity. As Thacker centers under the ball, he sees future visions of his unborn child. He sees a child waiting aimlessly in front of a picture window, searching for his father. Then he sees himself walking to the door of the home, being attacked with love by the child who calls him dad. The ball falls into Thacker's' glove and wakes him from his meditative state. "You're out!" the umpire shouts. "My God, he has done it fans!" Ray shouts. "Thacker is perfect!"

The crowd erupts as the players rush the mound to congratulate their hurler. Thacker looks into his glove in disbelief and falls to the ground on both knees with tears of joy streaming down his face. His teammates gather him up, with Fey leading the pack, as they lift him upon their shoulders to carry him off the field and into the clubhouse. Thacker looks back over at his wife but can't see her because of the sun's setting rays which are now beaming down the third base line of the field. He puts his cap in front of his eyes catching a glimpse of her eyes, giving him a warm sensation once again, but this time one of mere perfection.

The Great Escape

       Denver, Colorado is a gorgeous city during the winter time. The snow covered trees, the sun reflecting off the iced-covered lake, and the soaring mountains are perfect for snowboarding. Denver is the ideal place to spend my winter vacation. The cabin I am staying in is high in the mountains miles away from the nearest town. The cabin is peaceful, quiet, and serene, just the way I like it. Another cabin is off in the distance, approximately a football field length away from mine. I do not have a clue if anyone lives in the cabin; however, it looks desolate. I do not care too much about the cabin, but there is something that makes me curious about it.

       Over the next couple of days, I notice the weather is taking a turn for the worse. I tune in the radio to the local weather station to see how long this nasty weather is going to last. The meteorologist says, "blizzards are on the way, stock up on food and other supplies because the snow will cover over the roads and trails in the area." I layer on warm clothes, grab my Iditarod, and mush into town. The sun is shining, but the temperature is ice cold and the wind blows fiercely. I am having a difficult time seeing the trail because of the wind kicking up snow from every direction. I pull up on the reins so my dogs will slow down. We are approaching the frozen river we must cross to get into town. This is not my first trip over the frozen river, and I approach with both caution and confidence.

       I shout to the dogs "mush" and draw the whip back and smack it forward. The lead dog Alister always performs well in these tricky situations. Alister starts across with the other dogs following carefully behind. The wind is blowing harder and it is hard to hear anything over the sound. The crackling noise I hear is the wind as it whistles by my ears. Alister is safely across the river followed quickly by the other dogs and my sled.

       I quickly enter the store and stock up on food, firewood, and other miscellaneous items I think I need. I pack up the supplies in my sled and tie them down tight. After the supplies are secure, I organize the dogs and proceed back up the mountain to my cabin. The temperature is dropping fast, the wind is bitter, and nightfall is minutes away. We have to get to the cabin before nightfall or we are in trouble. I shout to the dogs to go faster and crack the whip. Finally I arrive at the cabin; I untie the dogs and let them inside. I unpack the supplies and throw wood into the fireplace. I am safe and sound in my cabin enjoying the warmth of the fire.

I walk to the window to see what the weather is doing. The cabin in the distance is lifeless and it has sparked my curiosity. I do not know what to do because if someone lives in the cabin they could be caught unaware of the dangerous weather quickly approaching. I decide to walk over to see if there is someone inside. I put on my warm clothes again and leave the warmth of the cabin to check on the neighbor. As I approach the cabin, I notice the door is slightly ajar. I knock and say, "Hello, anyone home?" There is no answer. I call out once more and still no answer. I walk inside and notice the cabin is not like mine. This cabin is much bigger inside with an upstairs and a basement. I explore the cabin just to make sure no one is inside.

First I check the upstairs; I then proceed to the main floor. I call out, "Is anyone here? Hello?" Still, there is no answer. I walk downstairs to the basement. The basement is dark, cold, and the stairs are old and creak with every step I take. I take out my pocket radio and say, "come in Mike. Mike come in." I wait for a reply. "eh Joe I am in the cabin. Where are you?" I tell Mike I am exploring the cabin across the way to make sure no one is staying there. Mike says, "Are you crazy with a blizzard on the way?" I tell Mike to come to the cabin to help me check out the basement. He responds, "I am on my way wuss. I will be there in five minutes." When Mike says five minutes it usually means ten. I told him to knock three times so I will know it is him.

I go over to the stairs and sit down and wait for Mike. I hear a light knock on the door, but something is not right. Mike would knock harder than that. He is a tall, hefty man, built like an ox but soft like a teddy bear. A minute passes and another knock just like the first. I grab my Colt 45, cock it back, and quietly approach the door. I unlock the dead bolt and turn the knob slowly. I open the door a crack hoping to trick whoever it is into coming in. The person yells, "Hello!" I slip out from behind the door and yell, "freeze"! The person turns around and says, "Joe, it is me, Mike". "Mike what in the hell were you thinking? I told you to knock three times not two. You nearly gave me a heart attack." He says sarcastically, "awe you poor baby". I give Mike a dirty look and say, "let's get going."

Mike and I go down to the basement because it is the last room we have left to check. We walk down the stairs and with our flashlights we look around. We try to find a light switch so we can get a better look at what is down here. Mike's flashlight suddenly goes out and mine starts to dim. "We have to find a light switch before your flashlight goes out too," Mike says. "Thank you captain obvious", I say sarcastically. We walk around staying close to the wall, feeling around hoping there is a light switch nearby. We hear a click noise coming from Mike's foot. We look at each other in terror knowing exactly what the click noise is. Mike has stepped on a mine and if he moves we will both be dead.

Mike and I plan what we can do about this situation and how to avoid getting killed. Mike tells me I need to find an object equal to his weight to keep the pressure down on the mine. I recall feeling a metal post when we were searching for a light switch. I tell Mike I will be right back and to not move a muscle. I retrace my steps and find the metal post. I lug it back to where Mike is and ask him, "will this work Mike or do I need to find something heavier"? Mike says, "we better hope it works or we will both be dead." I roll the metal post over to see how wide it is. Mike tells me that it will work just as long as I am careful.

Pressure is the key to success here. As long as there is pressure on the trigger at all times we will survive. If the pressure slips for a fraction of a second, we will both be dead. I put the metal close to Mike's feet; our timing has to be perfect. "When I say one…two…three lift, lift your foot," I say. Mike says, "I agree and start by counting to three then lift." I start counting, one…two…three…lift. Mike lifts his foot and I quickly shove the metal post under his foot.

Mike feels his face then feels mine and calls out, "we are alive…we are alive!" Mike gives me a tight bear hug and still we are in shock we are alive. I say, "Why are you so ecstatic Mike? You did not trust me did you?" "To be honest, no, I did not, but you did it," Mike replied. I just shake my head and walk on. We continue feeling up and down the wall trying to find the light switch. Mike calls out, "I think I found something over here Joe." Mike finds a candle that is on a metal platform. I pick up the candle and the floor gives way. The floor is booby trapped. Mike and I are on some type of short slide and going down fast. Mike exclaims, "Where is this taking us Joe"? "Like I know where this slide thing leads Mike. I have not been here before son", I replied. "Just hold on Mike we will get out of this", I said. Mike is a big burly guy; however, when it comes to things like this he is a scaredy cat.

I could finally see an opening in the distance hoping it was the end of the trap. "I can see the end, I think; Mike brace yourself for impact", I said. We were picking up speed and I jetted out first. Mike called out, "heads up Joe I'm coming". Mike comes soaring out of the trap flailing his arms up in the air. I did not have time to react so Mike landed on my abdomen. Mike sat up on me and said, "It is pretty nice down here". "I'm just loving being down here Mike; it brings a joy to my day", I replied sarcastically. "Oh sorry Joe didn't see you down there," Mike said with a smirk. We got up, brushed the cobwebs and dust off, and continued exploring.

Our heads were on a swivel as we walked down through the enormous room. A blinding light came out from nowhere. I called out to Mike, "what did you do this time Mike?" A booming deep voice rose and echoed throughout the area. The voice said, "What a pleasant surprise. The one and only Joey Roembke has graced us with his presence." I did not recognize the voice or know how this person behind the voice knew me. I replied, "Who are you? And what do you want from me?" Large chains busted out of the wall behind us. The chains gripped me around my wrists and ankles. Mike lunged after me but a huge cage and ring of fire enclosed him.

The bright light dimmed down and I could hear a noise off in the distance. The noise sounded like high heels hitting a wooden floor. The noise was getting closer and out of the darkness stood a man. The man stood about six feet tall; he wore an Ushanka made out of mink, a long fur trench coat, and his beard was mostly black, with a few grey hairs sprinkled in. He said, "Well...well... look what we have here." The man exaggerated his R's and had a heavy voice with a husky pitch. The medicinal smell of spoiled vodka lingered on his breath and pierced my nostrils. "Ever heard of a breath mint", I asked coughing. The man pulled his gun from his holster and hit me across the face saying, "Shut up!" I wiped the blood from my mouth and replied, "Who are you and what do you want from me?" The man took a drink of Vodka and said," I'm your worst nightmare friend. I have been hired to kill you". "You're an assassin? Really? Not buying it my friend," I said. The man punched me again and yelled with his nasty accent, "I will prove it to you. I'll be right back". The man turned around and disappeared into the darkness.

I called over to Mike, "How you doing over there?" Mike said with a wheezing voice, "I'm good besides the fact I am number one caged up like a wild creature and number two feeling like I'm standing on the sun. Other than those two minor things I'm peachy. How you holding up? That Russian handed you some vicious punches." "Yeah he has a gruesome right hook, but I'm hanging in there" I said chuckling. "On a serious note; we need to find a way out of here" I said. Mike said, "I know Joe, but how do you plan to do that? We are a miles up on top of a mountain, isolated from society, with no cell phone reception, and not to mention you're chained to a wall, a ring of fire is surrounding me and I'm locked in a cage !" I can hear a door unlatching in the distance and the sound of those boots coming. I shouted, "Hush Mike he is coming back."

The man came back and unlocked me from the chains that bound me to the wall, grabs a chair with no bottom, and pushed me down into it. He chains me to the chair and lays a folder stacked with papers and pictures down in front of me. The papers have information about me that no one else knows about. The folder also contains pictures of me doing daily activities. I said, "So you are for real eh?" "Yes my friend, I am and it is almost time for your life to end." he replies. The man walked over to the table types in some numbers and steps away. He says with a sinister look in his eyes, "It is an honor to be in your presence friend. I am sorry things had to end this way." "I'll see you soon", I said with a smirk.

The man walked out the door and locked it behind him. "That's a bomb Joe! A bomb!" Mike exclaimed. "Thank you captain obvious, I know what it is", I said. While Mike is panicking frantically I am trying to conjure up a plan to get us out of this sticky situation. I recall Mike having a laser on him because his overprotective mother gave him one just in case. I shout over to Mike, "hey Mike get yourself together and follow everything I am about to say. Do you understand me?" "Yes Joe, I understand." Mike said. "Okay good. Do you still have that laser pointer that your wonderful mother gave to you"? I say. Mike searches through his various pockets looking for his laser. Mike jumps up and down yelling," I found it! I found it!" I say, "Okay, now aim it steadily towards the chains, and cut them off." Mike aims the laser through the columns of the cage and slowly starts cutting the chains off my hands and ankles. The chains fall off my wrists and ankles hitting the floor with a loud clang. I look at the time ticking away on the bomb; we do not have much time, and I have to free Mike somehow. I hurriedly rush to free Mike from his imprisoned state. Mike calls out to me, "the switch and lever are behind me." I sprint over and find the switches. I pull up hard on the rusty lever lifting the cage, putting an end to the ring of fire. "We now have to find a way off this mountain," I say. "I know man but how? You know there will be an avalanche when the bomb ticks down to zero," Mike replies. We look around trying to find a way out of the building and down the mountain.

The bomb only has two minutes remaining before detonation. Mike calls over from across the room, "Hey Joe I think I found something over here". I head over Mike's way and I see a snowmobile with barely any gas, a rope and an old wooden snowboard. I say, "How is this going to help us get out of here alive?" "We'll fire up the snowmobile, tie the rope to the back and you will ride behind on the old wooden snowboard." Mike says with a grin on his face. I reply, "It's a long shot, but we have nothing to lose but our lives of course." I run over to see how many ticks are left on the bomb. "We have t minus 45 seconds till this place goes boom," I say.

I hear the rumbling sound of the snowmobile and put my feet into the straps of the snowboard. I stand up and give Mike the signal. Mike floors it and the snow mobile jerks me forward. Mike yells back, "Hold on tight we have to go over this gnarling slop." The building explodes behind Mike and me. The sight is beautiful but it unlashes a deadly avalanche that is coming for us. I feel like we are in a James Bond movie for a second flying down the mountain with a building exploding behind us. I snap out of that daydream real quick. I can sense the avalanche is getting closer. I can hear the vast suffocating rush of the avalanche just behind us. The roar of the wave is getting closer and closer. I call out to Mike, but I realize it is no use; the echoing of the avalanche is too loud.

I heard an unfamiliar sound ringing in my ears. The sound lasted only for a slight second then it went off. I felt a pain in my arm like someone was pushing at me from the side. Then I heard a boom and someone called out, "wake up!" I opened my eyes and standing before me was my eighth period teacher shaking her head. I asked, "What happened?" My teacher said, "well you and your buddy Mike slept through my lecture today. I will see you both in detention the Monday after winter break."

I turned around and Mike stood smirking at me. We grabbed our bags and started out the door. I said to Mike, "bro I just had the craziest dream about you and me. You wouldn't even believe me if I told you." Mike replied sarcastically, "oh, you did? I couldn't care less Joe I'm ready to go up to the cabin in Denver tonight." I just smiled and said, "me too, Mike, but promise me one thing. If there is a blizzard while we are up there, talk me out of going across to the other cabin alright?" "You're one crazy man Joe, but alright bro I'll talk you out of it if this so called "blizzard" ever occurs," Mike said as he rolled his eyes. I just smiled mumbled under my breath, "this winter vacation could be like a James Bond movie." Mike said, "what did you say?" I said laughing, "nothing just get in the car Mike." We both got in and headed for Denver.

Runaway

I was six when I ran away. I do not recall what caused me to leave home. However, I remember feeling unwanted and neglected. One chilly fall day, my mom was busy with other things and not paying any attention to me. Nothing I could do drew her attention away from her household duties that day. She continued to cook breakfast, watch her Lifetime movie, and complain about how tough life was. I could not get her attention with my whining, fussing, or demands. When mom called me for breakfast, I told her, "Mom I am running away from home". I was hoping she would stop me but she just ignored me. I figured if I ran away she would sooner or later miss me.

Gary, one of my favorite uncles, told me a story about how he ran away from home for a couple of days. In the end, his parents found him and it all turned out just fine. I filled up a backpack with a pillow, clothes, a blanket, snacks, and other things I thought I needed. Later in the night I crept out the back door. The tree house was perfect. It was hidden but still close to home. The leaves of the tree made it easier to hide from my mom if she came looking for me.

The first night I succeeded in hiding out. No one came looking for me. The next morning I walked next door to my aunt and uncle's house and had breakfast with them. I made up an excuse why I was over there so early in the morning. I told them that I just stopped over for a visit and they believed me. My cover was not blown. It was time to carry out the next step of my fantabulous run away from home plan. I took the back way from my aunt's and uncle's house so I was not spotted by anyone. I had to get past barking dogs, giant water puddles, and a pond covered in green muck. Using my secret ninja skills, I arrived at my destination without being seen.

The next day was even better because all my meals were delivered to me. My friend, Chris, lived down the street. I texted him, told him what I was doing, and asked if he could help me out. He told me I was crazy for doing this but, after a little charm and acting pitiful, he agreed to help me. He brought me food from his house. He put it in a bucket at the bottom of the tree house and I pulled it up. My mom never noticed Chris because he was trained in the ninja arts just like I was. I was living the life up in my tree house. I thought I was invincible like every other boy my age. I was feeling a bit overconfident, and this was my downfall.

The third night a terrible storm hit. I was not expecting the rain but you know what they say, "expect the unexpected." The storm was nasty bringing a lot of rain, high winds, and golf-ball size hail. The tree house had an inner portion where I could normally avoid getting wet. The high winds were blowing the rain in all directions, and I was soaking wet. Another mother, Mother Nature, decided to foil my plans to stay in the tree house. I grabbed what I could carry, as quickly as possible, and went back home.

My mom questioned my whereabouts the last three days. She said she had been looking everywhere for me. I told her I ran away and camped out in the tree house. I explained I did it because she made me feel unwanted. Mom pulled me in tight and whispered in my ear three little words I will never forget, "Joey, you're grounded!"

Hopeless

My eyes are swollen. I can't see. Tears run down my face. My nose drips with blood. I must be stupid. I must be bad. What else could've made my dad so mad? I wish I could be different. I wish I could be everything he wants me to be. Maybe then my life would be better. If I was the perfect child, my mom would still want to hug me. I can't speak. I can't do anything right. If I do something wrong, they'll lock me up in my room. No light. No food. No bed. Just me and the cold hard floor. My room becomes a jail cell. I stay silent. I write down everything that happens to me in my journal. When my mom comes in, I try to be nice - - really do, but it's no use. She whips me like a slave. I stay quiet. I do not make a sound. The belt snaps into my back repeatedly.

I hear a car. Its dad, he's back from Charley's Bar. I hear him curse as he shouts my name. I press myself against the wall. I pull my knees tight up close to my face. Tears run faster down my face. I try to hide myself from his piercing evil eyes, but it's no use. He grabs my neck and chokes me. I am afraid. I am helpless. I am hopeless. I cry harder. When he sees me crying, he shouts hateful things. He says it's my fault that he suffers at work. He slaps me hard across the face. The noise from his cold rough hand on my face echoes through my gloomy, empty room. He continues to yell louder. I break free from his unforgiving grip and run for the door, but it's already locked. Once again I break down and bawl. He grabs my arm and throws me into the wall. I fall heavily on the hard wooden floor. My body, mind, and spirit feel broken. "I'm sorry!" I scream, but it's far too late. His expression has already turned into one of an unbearable hate. I feel vulnerable and powerless, like a newborn baby. My body hurts. The pain increases. I scream, "God have mercy, please let it end!" I lay motionless, sprawled on the harsh unyielding floor, as he heads for the door.

The Green Scarf

My mom was a beautiful and smart woman. I always called her a nerd because I thought she dressed funny. My mom always became sensitive when the subject came up about her job. Whenever we referred to her place of employment, we just called it "the green scarf." We moved around every two years or so for her job. This made me a little suspicious because she told me that the Defense Department stays stationary.

As I grew older, I became more curious. One day when I was about 10 years old, I stood before her, hands on hips, and asked what exactly "the green scarf" was. She said she was a nurse in the Army. I pictured her as the nurse answering to an injured soldier on the battle field, putting her own life in danger to save those brave men. She did not answer my original question, but I learned something new about her. It didn't register that I had never actually seen her in a uniform. I wanted to believe her, and so I did.

Not long after, she changed her story. "I'm with the Defense Department," I overheard her tell someone over the phone. What happened to the Army? The Defense Department wasn't something I could imagine. I had no images of what it did. I saw a blank screen, but I didn't ask my mother to explain. Over the next couple of years, her job description continued to shift. The Defense Department became the State Department, then the Pentagon. Her titles as an advisor rotated even when we didn't move. Each time she rolled out a new cover story, she did so with perfectly still eyes. That's what made me think she wasn't switching jobs as much as switching titles, but if I suspected she wasn't exactly telling the truth, I was in no way ready to admit she was lying.

My awakening to the truth came during one of our weekly Sunday drives. At 12, I loathed being trapped inside an automobile with my parents and younger sister, but Sunday drives were a family obligation. That day, as my dad guided our Caprice Classic down the driveway, something didn't seem right. My father wasn't commenting on the well-groomed lawns, and my mother seemed more restrained than usual. Did they have a fight? I stared out the window, vaguely aware of the strange mood in the car, when unprompted, my father turned to my mother and growled, "tell the girls what you do for a living." My mother's neck stiffened. "I'm a supervisor," she mumbled feebly. "I manage people." Irritated, my father whirled around, his eyes mocking, and asked, "Do you girls have any questions for your mother about her work 'managing people'?" I loved the tone in his voice just then. It was a tone that refused to settle, a tone that said, I have had enough of your secrets. I didn't know why my father had chosen to confront my mother just then and still don't. Maybe he was tired of keeping her secret and of how it stifled their relationship and constrained our whole family.

Regardless, his nerve cheered me, so I assailed my mother with questions and tried to pin her down to specifics as she clung desperately to abstract generalities. Finally, my father narrowed his eyes and said, "You work for the CIA, don't you?" I didn't have any real sense of what the CIA was, just a Hollywood version of it, as the world of spies.

My mother said nothing. Staring straight ahead, he gripped the steering wheel as if it was all that kept him from flying from the car. My father knew my mother was in the CIA, of course he had to have known, but instead of saying anything more, he dropped the subject as abruptly as he had brought it up. For a moment, the door had cracked open and I had learned the truth: My mother was a "spy" for the CIA. I was flabbergasted but, at the same time, unable to square my dull mother with images of 007. None of us pursued the subject that day, or the following day, week or month. Over time, that moment faded almost entirely, until it became a dream, something I only half-believed.

During the next four years, our family disintegrated. My father, who had been diagnosed with cancer, tried his best but wasn't able to beat the disease. After he died, I continued to march from school to home and back again like the soldier I was raised to be. I finished high school, applied to college and moved to Boston.

While I was in college, my mother moved again, this time to central Virginia. The summer of my sophomore year I went "home" to visit her. My mother drove me through unfamiliar, remote parts of Virginia, turned onto a wooded road and pulled to a stop at an unassuming cinder-block gatehouse. I sat in the car while my mother got out discussing something with a uniformed guard at the gatehouse. I was disoriented. Where exactly were we? When the guard motioned for me to get out of the car, I stepped out into the oppressive, muggy heat of that June day. Somewhere in the distance, popping sounds shattered the air like firecrackers. I looked down the road and thought "guns," but said nothing.

The guard ushered me into the low-lying brick building. Once inside, he lifted a clipboard from his desk and said matter-of-factly, "This is a CIA base. Everyone who lives here and their guests must sign a form stating they will not disclose this information to anyone." His words rang across the silence that had intervened since that Sunday drive. After endless shifting cover stories, I finally had confirmation of the truth. It didn't matter that it was a stranger telling me. It only mattered that I knew. I felt betrayed. All my life, my mother had lied to me.

It was freeing to hear the truth, but like that Sunday in the car, this moment too was short-lived. The guard stood before me, clipboard in hand, waiting for my signature. After I signed, the guard took a picture of me for the badge I would show coming and going from the "home" I could tell no one about. My mother's secret was mine now.

That was more than 20 years ago. In that time, I came to understand why my mother had to lie. Our relationship has improved and is still evolving as we talk more and more. She has since retired and, because she wanted to teach, has gone through a process controlled by the agency to remove her covers and change her status from covert to overt. She's now happy to share her secret of having been in the CIA. She teaches, gives interviews and lectures, and has appeared on the History Channel. She'll openly talk about her job now. She explained to me the title of her work. The operation she was spying on was called "green scarf" because the target was always wearing a green scarf. I sarcastically said, "the CIA is very creative".

After keeping my mother's secret for so long, I'm free to disclose it. Yet, to this day, I still can't help but feel like I'm betraying her every time I say, "My mother worked for the CIA." I, to this day, give my mom credit for keeping this whole "green scarf" operation a secret from me.

The Hazard

The final day of the World Champion Golf Tournament was coming to a close. The look of exhaustion fell over the final players. One and a half million dollars was on the line, and a beautiful seven foot tall golden trophy with all the previous winners would go home with the winner as well. The players have put up a tough fight tying each other on every hole and not showing any signs of weakness. The most hated hole, hole eighteen, would decide the winner. The eighteenth hole was playing harder than any other hole on the course. The rain dancing on the green making it soft and luscious. The smooth but furious wind was making the players think twice about club choice, and the cold bitter temperature was taking its toll on the players. The gallery hurried to seventeen's fairway to see the final players battle it out for first place. The spectators were bundled up, wearing heavy kelly-green rain jackets; long grey pants that barely passed the knee were worn and were accompanied by thick wool red and green plaid socks. The caddies carried umbrellas over the two golfers as they walked to the eighteenth tee box. The crowd roared in excitement and applauded as the players walked between them.

Luke Banks was the number one golfer in the world. Banks had won twelve championships, four majors, and the masters twice. However, Banks has never won at Saint Andrews before. Banks was about six foot, two inches tall. His long cinder block like arms bulged from his dark purple shirt. He was a barrel chested man with flexible rounded-shoulders. The veins in his wide, rough hands popped out as he planted the tee into the ground. His unshaven face pulled more attention to his bright green eyes. He stood next to his caddy and placed his long finger and thumb upon his chin. His caddy was a scrawny man, no more than five feet tall. He wore a purple and pink argyle sweater; his navy blue pants were ironed to perfection. He wore big black framed glasses; he had on a blue bucket hat with Banks' name stitched on the rim. He did not look strong; however, when he lifted up Banks' bag the veins in both biceps came alive. They stood foot to foot and mumbled a couple of words back and forth. The wind was picking up, the rain came down harder, and the temperature was dropping by the minute.

Hole eighteen was a lengthy 530 yard par five. The fairway doglegged to the left side and then turned back. The right side was filled with mile-high bunkers and long, wild fescue. The bunkers were low but had a steep incline making them difficult to hit out of. The fescue was long, thick, and untamed. An old Scottish mansion ran along the left side of the fairway. The mansion was 8,000 square feet and was beautiful. The front of the mansion faced towards the eighteenth green. The whole mansion was created with tan, rough stones. A long stone staircase with worn down iron handrails lead down to the eighteenth green. This mansion was owned by the president of Saint Andrews. The president was sitting down with his wife on the front porch. The president wore a simple, plain navy blue suit with golden buttons. Underneath he wore a forest green shirt which was accompanied by a blue and green plaid bowtie. He had small square shaped sliver rimmed glasses on. He wore long navy pants, tan saddle oxfords on his feet, and plaid socks to match his bowtie. In his suit pocket sat a kelly-green pocket square folded in a Triple Crown design. He would make a movement every minute; he could not sit still. He would constantly cross then uncross his legs. His huge hands were blue and black in color. His hands, for some odd reason, would not stop shaking back and forth. He looked through the binoculars that were hanging from his neck, so he could watch Banks tee off.

"Quiet please Quiet!" said the manager.

The scrawny caddy handed Banks the club and whispered some words into Banks' ear. Banks shook his head in agreement and stepped up to the tee box. Banks stood behind the ball and observed the winding fairway. His bright green eyes zoomed in on a little patch of fairway just before a fairway bunker. Banks took a deep breath in and then exhaled out. He lined up his four iron to the ball, separated his legs shoulder-width apart, looked up at the fairway once more, and then started his back swing. His hips pivoted back towards the gallery and the iron whipped up into the air. His hips moved in a forward motion as he began his down swing. His hands flew through the ball and the iron made solid contact with the ball, sending it high into the dark gloomy sky.

"Get in the hole!" A man's voice from the gallery shouted.

Banks held his follow through and watched the ball as it started to fade toward the bunker.

"Sit, Sit Boo Boo! Sit!" Banks shouted in disgust.

The ball trickled down into the bunker and Banks shoved his four iron into his bag. Banks mumbled some words to his caddie once more.

Banks looked at someone in the crowd and mouthed, "it's ok. I have this under control."

I knew something was wrong; I had followed Banks throughout the years, and he was not strong like the man who hit the tee shot.

I heard a spectator next to me say, "I don't ever remember seeing Banks get mad before and throw clubs; I also do not remember him having that body type. His arms are like cinder blocks. That bloody bastard has to be on roids".

Maybe this spectator was right. The man won the world championship and greeted the president with his golden trophy.

"I knew the switch a-rue would work my boy; I knew it. Good work out there" whispered the president.

When the man claiming to be Banks walked into the men's locker room, I followed him close.

"Who are you? The real you? I know what you did and where is the real Banks?" I asked.

He started to run away knowing I was onto him.

"Stop! Stop!" I called while tackling him to the ground.

"Get off me! Get off me! You're breaking my arm" He cried out.

"Who are you? Just tell me?" I simply said.

"I'm Eric Sexton number one golfer in the US. Banks was sick and I covered for him. You can't tell a soul!" He responded

"Get up. I won't if you give me half the money" I said with a smirk.

He rolled his eyes and struggled, then said, "Fine I'll give you a cut, but you can't tell a soul".

"That's a deal" I said, shaking his hand.

Little did Mr. Sexton know I was taping the whole conversation with the tape recorder I carried in my pocket.

"That's how your daddy got to live here son. All because I observed something that was out of place". I said to my son rubbing my fingers through his curly hair.

"Wow dad that's crazy. You're the best dad ever!" My son said.

"Thanks son. Now I will read you a bedtime story. Go to bed. We have golf in the morning. Goodnight son. Love you", I said shutting out the light and shutting the door behind me.

Summer's Favorite Pastime

As a teenager, summertime fun in the sun begins with the ringing of the last school bell of the year. It signifies time to throw away old homework assignments and forget about school for the next three months. Summer is a time for excitement and simple pleasures. The ideal summer is three months of late nights with friends, laying by the pool with girls, and of course, baseball.

The day starts early to catch the 8:00 a.m. train to Chicago. With ice cold milk in hand, I think about the events, hopes and wishes for today's game. I overhear other passengers commenting, "Maybe someone will hit a homerun," and "I hope the Cubs win today". The train is pulling up to Ogilvie Station, and I am one step closer to the game.

The short taxi ride to the ballpark takes far longer than it should due to the hundreds of cars and buses assaulting the streets. As the taxi creeps along, Wrigley Field slowly climbs out of the Chicago skyline. Wrigley Field is a beautiful sight to behold. I am in awe every time I see the stadium. I drift off into my own mind imagining all of the players and the history made in this famous place. I pay the taxi driver, and I am off to the game. The striking red brick of the building, the bold green ivy lazily climbing its walls, and the "WRIGLEY FIELD, Home of the CHICAGO CUBS" sign scrolling across the entrance to the stadium is unreal. I cannot believe I am here. A smile slowly tiptoes across my face. I am unsure if this jubilation is because of the look of the ballpark or the realization that game time is getting closer.

The day's weather is perfect for a baseball game. The temperature is 75°, the sun is shining, and there is a light breeze coming in from the north. As I enter the ballpark, all the energy is unbelievable. The people next to me are arguing about which is the better team, a guy is yelling "programs, get your programs here", and little boys are asking their dads questions about baseball in general. The crowd decked out in their red, white, and blue is something extraordinary to see.

I travel up ten flights of stairs and finally arrive at my seat. Wrigley Field is shaped like the coliseum in Rome; there is no such thing as a bad seat. The circular layout makes it convenient to see the game from any angle. The outfield walls are made of brick and covered in ivy, which is unique to Wrigley Field. I hear the announcer say, "throwing the ceremonial first pitch is Barry Larkin". The crowd roars loudly, and everyone rises to their feet to give Barry a standing ovation. I know at this point there is no place in the world like Wrigley Field.

The noise from the crowd dies down a bit as the announcer says, "Please rise for the playing of our National Anthem." I do not know who is singing the anthem, but her voice is angelic. As she sang, goosebumps appear on my arms, fireworks shoot up in the air, and three fighter jets fly overhead. I hear the fans yell "play ball"! The game is finally underway.

Food vendors are walking up and down the stairs calling out "Get your hotdogs, cold root beer, and cracker jacks here". I shout, "I'll take a drink and a hotdog please". There is nothing like a ballpark hotdog and an ice cold root beer. The crowd cheers and gets into the spirit of the game.

The game is less than exciting for the first eight innings. Both teams come into the ninth inning scoreless. It is the bottom of the ninth with two outs and runners on the corners. The crowd rises to their feet as the hometown hero steps to the plate for the first time. Standing an impressive six feet, seven inches tall and weighing 250 pounds, he appears formidable with tattoos on both arms, his muscles bulging and chewing tobacco in his mouth. He spits out a wad of tobacco, steps in the batter's box, and taps the plate with his bat.

The first pitch is a fast ball, traveling at 101 miles per hour right down the middle for strike one. The second pitch is another fast ball down the middle, traveling at the speed of 100 miles per hour for strike two. I could feel the energy level in the ballpark drop like a rock. The pitcher nods to the catcher. It seems like slow motion as the pitcher reaches back and delivers the pitch. The hometown hero steps forward and swings, but misses the pitch for strike three. I am speechless. Just when his team needs him the most the hometown hero does not deliver the win. The crowd is in shock as the game goes into extra innings. The Cubs pull out the win with an out- of- the park homerun in the bottom of the eleventh inning.

I think about the hometown hero and how he must be feeling. His team came back with a win; however, he did not capitalize on his chance at bat. I recall something my high school coach said to our team after a really tough loss. He said, "Baseball is a game of failure, and we cannot win them all." I really did not understand what he meant by that at the time. Watching this game helped me understand what he meant. There will be another game and another chance to swing the bat. The hometown hero will hopefully be able to connect when that time comes.

It is time to leave the ballpark for a long ride home. I am thinking about the game today and the summer days yet to come. I know there will be homeruns like sunny days with friends and strike outs when it rains or I have to work. In the end, summer will always be a winner.

Blue-Eyed Woman

Paris in the fall, what a beautiful city; it's a wonderful place to be. This city is full of culture with its famous landmarks and mysterious air about it. One can have wondrous adventures in this city of lights. On this day in Paris, the sun is shining and the air is crisp, a perfect fall day. The city bustles with activities, and the Eiffel tower is full of tourists. The Louvre is still one of the most interesting places in the city with all of its wonderful treasures like Leonardo da Vinci's "Mona Lisa". Just looking at the painting gives me a warm feeling. Looking into her eyes I get the impression there is a secret hidden away, hmmm…intriguing.

After leaving the Louvre, I strolled through the city looking at the people as they pass by; it is amazing what I see when I take the time to look. As I walked along, I stop because a strikingly beautiful woman catches my eye. Just under her hood lays her raven black hair. Her eyes are as blue as the sky; and she walks so elegantly down the street. I have to catch up with this lovely woman; she is too stunning to be let go. My palms were sweaty, my knees start to become weak, and my cheeks quickly become flushed like red roses. I have never been this nervous in my entire life. The woman walks into a building before I can catch up with her. My French is rusty; it has been awhile since I have spoken it, and I cannot make out the name of the building. I decide to walk in after her thinking to myself, "What the heck, it couldn't hurt. Right?"

I grab the gold handle of the door, pull it open, and proceed inside. The building is massive; it consists of many hallways leading to different parts of the building and has crystal chandeliers hanging from the ceiling. The ceiling has famous paintings depicted on them like the Vatican. I do not know where all these hallways lead or what this building is used for. I lost sight of the beautiful woman. I decide to exit the building and wait until the woman comes out.

I take a seat on the bench right outside the door and begin reading my book. Hours pass by, and the sun is beginning to set over the horizon. My eyes are becoming heavy; I am struggling to stay awake. The woman has not yet come out of the building. I am at a loss about what I should do next. I slump down on the bench and wait a little while longer. An hour passes and the massive doors finally creaked open. The woman finally walks out, and here is my opportunity. I move toward the woman and simply say, "Bonjour madam". She turns and faces me with those stunning blue eyes and responds, "Bonjour monsieur que puis-je faire pour vous? I do not know what she is asking of me. I ask, "Parlez-vous anglais?" The woman still has an accent when she responds, "Yes I do". The accent is difficult to pinpoint, but I can clearly understand her. I ask her where she is headed and if I can accompany her. She indicates yes by a nod of her head, and we head down the street.

I start asking the woman simple questions just to strike up a conversation. "What's your name? If you don't mind me asking". "I don't mind one bit. I'm Gabriella. Who are you?" she asked. "Raymond" I say. "Raymond huh? You live around here?" "I do not. I live in the United States. I'm just visiting part of my family who lives here. How about you? Where are you from?" She replies, "I'm from Spain originally but came to Paris to follow my dream of being a ballerina." "Well you have beauty and grace going for you already," I say with a smile. She blushes and says, "Thank you, you are too kind." I say, "Just telling the truth miss." She smiles and her cheeks become red like roses. We finally arrive at our destination where she is staying. "Thank you for keeping me company on the way home Ray." she says. I respond with a half-smile, "Ray, okay, making nicknames I see. It is my pleasure. No problem at all." She responds with that sweet voice of hers, "Goodnight". "When will I be able to see you again?" I ask nervously. She says, "How does tomorrow at 8:00 o'clock in the morning sound? We can get coffee or something?" "I would like that. I'll pick you up around 7:30 then", I said. She just smiles and walks in the door.

It is a long walk back to my place, but the night is perfect. The moon is shining, a slight breeze is blowing in from the north, and the sky is so clear every star is in sight. The Eiffel tower looks incredible at night. The tower is draped in bright lights which reflect off the bay close by. The walk seems to be longer than I expect probably because I am getting lost in the stunning scenery. I arrive home and discover my aunt had left the lights on for me. I grab the key under the mat, put it in the lock and walk in. I put my coat on the rack quietly and tip-toed up the old wooden stairs. No matter how quiet I try to be, it is no use because the stairs still make a crackling racket with each step. I arrive at the top of the stairs and proceed down the hallway to my room.

I quietly make my way down the hallway. The flooring is carpeted, so I assume it will not make noise. I am almost to my room when I hear a loud screech arise from down the hallway. I do not see any lights on anywhere in the house so I keep on walking. I hear a strange noise coming from behind me and I turn around and yell, "Aunt Jan, it is me!" She lowers the Louisville slugger she has in her hand and says, "You scared the hell out of me Raymond". "I thought you knew I was coming that is why the light was left on", I say. She says, "No your uncle Gary forgot to turn it off". I shrug my shoulders and say, "Well I am sorry for the scare Jan. I am heading to my room and bed. I will talk to you tomorrow morning". "That sounds wonderful", she says heading back into her room.

I head to my room, set the alarm for 6:00 A.M., shut the blinds, and pull the covers over my head. The sun creeps through the cracks of the blinds, morning is finally here. I am five minutes ahead of schedule for once. I throw back the covers, grab my clothes, and hop into the shower. I dry off and then go into the extra bathroom because the mirror is steamed up from the hot water. I brush my teeth, shave, put wax in my hair to give it a little extra pop, tie my bowtie and head out the door.

I arrive at Gabriella's just in the nick of time. I walk up to the front door and knock. Gabriella somehow looks even more beautiful than she did the day before. Her hair is straightened and curls at the bottom. It flows in waves to adorn her glowing porcelain-like skin. Her eyes, framed by long lashes, are a bright baby blue and seem to brighten the world; she seems the picture of perfection. Gabriella is wearing a hot red dress with heels that are as white as snow. She has a pearl necklace on and red lipstick on to match her dress. I pull the rose from my back pocket and give it to her and say, "Wow, You look wonderful". She smells the rose, smiles at me, gives my bowtie a little tug and responds, "Thank you. You're looking dapper yourself." "You ready to go?" I ask. "Yes I am; let's get going". I open the car door for her, she gets in, and we are on our way.

Gabriella and I go on many more dates over the next few weeks. We really start clicking. I bring her a single red rose every time we meet. I tell her I do not give a woman a dozen roses unless I'm going to ask her to marry me. Gabriella put her hand gracefully under her chin and didn't speak a word for a while. I ask, "Is something wrong?" She smiles and says, "Nope I'm just thinking about things". "What are you thinking about?" I ask eagerly. She says "Nothing!" I say, "Okay" and quickly change the subject. "Are we still on for tomorrow dinner at my place? I have something special planned." I say with a smirk. She says happily "Yes sir I will be there for sure. I can't wait". I walk her home later that day and kiss her on the forehead and say, "I'll see you tomorrow". She says, "OK drive home safe." I jump into my car, roll down the windows and wave goodbye to her.

I have a lot of things to do before Gabriella comes over. I have to clean and dust the house. I have to go shopping to buy the ring, pick up a dozen roses, and get all the recipes from my aunt so I can cook her favorite foods. I go to get the ring first. The clerk says it is beautiful and that any woman would love it. I say thank you to him and proceed down the street to the flower shop. I tell the store clerk my name and she retrieves the roses from the back. She brings the roses out and everything is perfect, just how I want it. I say "Thank you; they look great", and I run quickly to my car.

I arrive home minutes later and begin to make a list of things I need to get done. Sleep is the first thing on the list of course. I go up to bed as I am too tired to finish the list. I set the alarm for seven a.m. I roll over and fall asleep. "Ring" "Ring" "Ring"! I roll over and shut off the alarm. The day is finally here. I rush downstairs, grab the cleaning supplies and get to work. I clean every inch of my aunt and uncle's house, triple checking everything. Everything has to be perfect or as close to perfect as possible. I go into the kitchen and drape the table in a white table cloth, put two candles on the table, and stick the roses in a vase in the middle of the table. I put the finest plates, forks, spoons, and knives on the table for this special event. Everything is perfect. The food is almost done, and I have an hour to get ready.

I rush upstairs, put my favorite song on the speaker, and grab my favorite clothes. I hop into the shower singing my favorite song out loud. I wash up, and attempt to do my hair before I get out. I run my fingers through it, wax it and then blow it dry. I put on my slacks, button up my shirt, lace up my saddle oxfords, and tie my bowtie. I am ready to go.

Finally the doorbell rings and Gabriella is just on time. I tug on my bowtie, take a deep breath and open the door. I say "Hello Miss. How are you? Come on in." She says, "I'm good thanks. Something smells delicious." "I have your favorite meal cooking in the kitchen. Chicken Parmesan," I say smiling. She says, "How'd you know that was my favorite?" I respond "I know things blues eyes. I know things." She just giggles and says "You're good. A little too good". I laugh then grab her hand and lead her into the kitchen.

I pull her seat out for her and serve her my famous chicken parmesan. She takes a bite and sees the roses on the table with the ring attached to it. I say "What do you say? Will you marry me?" She has tears running from her blue eyes and says, "Yes. Yes. It will be an honor". I walk over, pick her up, kiss her and say the most powerful words in the world "I love you." "I love you too silly," she says. We go into the living room turn on our favorite movie, cuddle close and fall asleep on the couch.

Gabriella and I move back to the United States later that week. She moves in with me days before the wedding. I know this is what love is. I took a chance and it paid off. Gabriella and I are celebrating our 52nd anniversary. I am falling for her all over again every day. She is truly my better half. There is not another woman on this planet I would rather spend my life with than her.

Mondays

The sun light peeked through my bedroom window. The start of a brand new day was here. I went downstairs, brewed a cup of coffee then grabbed the paper. Every Monday I go get the morning paper I see my neighbor with a long box. I do not know what the box holds within it or why he always has it on Mondays of all days. People are disgusted with Monday, me included. I proceeded back into the house and called up to my wife,

"Honey the man across the street is carrying that long box again".

She yelled back, "What's in the box and why does he have it every Monday?"

"I don't know babe. I want to find out, but I don't want to be nosey however." I said.

"Get to work Ray; you are going to be late. Love you. Have a good day." She responded.

"I'll see you when I get home. Love you too." I said.

I grabbed my trench coat, wrapped the scarf around my neck, and went on my way.

My firm is two miles away from my house. As I was walking, all I could think about was what's in that box. Why Monday's? There is nothing great about Mondays, so why would he pick Mondays. The thought of what was in the box just ate away at me the whole day. I don't know why it bothered me so much, but it did. I tried to focus on the cases on my desk, but I couldn't; the question was eating away at me like a guilty conscience. I finally completed my cases for the day and headed home. It was going on six o'clock, and the man next door was out watering his flowers. This is my chance to finally ask him what he carries in the box every Monday. Here goes nothing I thought to myself. Finally, I will get all my questions answered.

"Excuse me sir," I said politely

His aged skin was molded into an almost permanent scowl. Years of unhappiness were etched by every deep line and wrinkle on his face. His pensive eyes never focused on anything as he seemed to be permanently lost deep into his thoughts and unhappiness.

His lips were slightly turned down and his forehead had deep creases that pulled his eyebrows down, as if he were glaring. He appeared constantly angry with the melancholy that washed over him. He wore a gray wool cardigan with enlarged brown buttons. His pants were gray dress pants with patches where they had been poorly sewn. He wore black socks with black and gray saddle Oxfords that had rips in the toe.

"Yes. What do you want?" He said.

His voice was harsh and rough.

"I notice you carry a box with you every Monday." I said again nicely

"Yeah so what if I do? What's it to you?" He responded harshly.

I put aside his harshness remembering it was a Monday and everyone is somewhat cranky on Monday.

"I was just wondering what's in the box and why do you only have it on Monday?" I responded.

"I have been married for forty seven-years if you didn't know." He said with a lighter more relaxed tone.

"I didn't know that sir." I said.

"Well in the box I have flowers; a bouquet of roses. I give them to my wife every Monday. I have been giving them to her every single Monday for forty-seven years. I have not missed one Monday. You want to know something else. I do it because no one likes Mondays, so I brighten up her day and make her Monday not so terrible."

"Thank you for your time sir and thank you for answering my questions; I was just curious." I said while walking away waving.

"You're welcome. Remember, Mondays aren't all bad; you just have to add a little color and new life into it." He called out.

The man at first was a little harsh but lightened up a bit. His outlook on Mondays is unique to say the least. Adding color and new life to a day of the week is just unheard of, but he is right. If people do something different on Mondays then Mondays would not be so terrible. When I told my wife about the old man, she started cry. I want to know how after all these years he still remembers to buy his wife flowers every single

Monday, and he has not left one Monday out in forty-seven years. He is brightening up Mondays with the simplest thing on earth, a flower.

Midnight Snack

My parents took a trip to Florida during the first week of summer. They left me home alone for the entire week, which was peaceful and quiet. Because I was bored, I called up some friends and asked them to come over and spend the night. They came over but fell asleep at 9:00 p.m. I found myself bored again, so I decided to walk downstairs to get a snack.

My house was very old, and the stairs creaked with every step I took. I tried to be quiet because I didn't want to wake my friends who fell asleep downstairs. I felt like the quieter I tried to be the louder I was actually being. Arriving at my destination without waking up my friends, I slowly drew open the refrigerator door. Squinting as the light from the door pierced the darkness, I searched for a late night snack to sustain me until morning.

The house was abnormally quiet that night. I could usually hear the gentle whir of the freezer, but not that night. There was a tap on the glass window, followed by another. Rain began to dance on the gravel outside, and the trees seemed to whisper as a breeze blew through their branches. I smiled to myself; I have always loved summer rainstorms. Food in hand, still half blind in the darkness, I fumbled through the house, making my way back to my bedroom.

As I settled into bed and pulled my warm covers over me, I felt crumbs from my sandwich fall to the sheets. I just grinned to myself; I was both too hungry and too tired to care. Suddenly, the darkness of my bedroom was interrupted by a flash of lightning, illuminating my room through my window. I thought nothing of it at first, but then it happened again. Quickly I arose from the comfort of my bed and went to investigate.

A noise coming from the window in the family room caught my attention. I passed the window but dropped to my knees as a sharp pain shot through my foot. Reaching for the pain, I discovered a small shard of glass embedded there. As I removed the glass from my foot, I heard a growling sound coming from just outside the door.

Terrified, I leaped back at the sound of something pounding angrily on the door. I didn't want to look, but I had to find out what was outside.

Turning fearfully towards the window, I found myself eye to eye with a creature so hideous it defied description. With an evil grin, it turned and vanished into the dark and stormy night. My heart pounded out of my chest at 100 miles per hour. Sweat rolled down my panicked face. I pulled myself together and put a tarp over the shattered window. I walked through the house again and crawled back into bed.

Morning came and I rushed downstairs to tell my friends what had happened. My friends must be heavy sleepers because, as I told the story, they were shocked they did not hear a peep all night. We decided we had to find out what this thing was and stop it before it hurt someone. We formulated a plan to catch the creature I had seen.

The plan was simple; we would put a giant trip wire across the yard. The trip wire would result in an enormous cage falling from the trees and trap the creature. We grabbed our gear, plenty of food, and made our final adjustment to the trap. The tree house was the perfect camp site in view of the whole yard.

We waited for hours searching for this creature, but no activities were going on in the yard. It was so quiet outside we could hear a pin drop from miles away. My friends and I were sure this night was bust, but then we heard a bang almost as if someone shot a gun. We quickly grabbed the binoculars and ran to our post to see if the creature had come back. Jack spotted something about a mile away from our house. It was too far away to make out what exactly it was. One thing was certain, it was large and bulky.

We jumped out of the tree house and quickly and quietly snuck through the yards trying to get a better view of the creature. We hid behind an electric box praying that the creature would not see us. The creature hid in the shadows, and we could barely make out his imposing height, red eyes, blood covered-skin, and the smell of human flesh emanating from him. Brad pulled his camera from his bag and took a picture of this unusual and unsightly creature. The flash from the camera caught the creature's attention, and he spotted us.

Wasting no time, we sprinted away as fast as possible. The monster was chasing after us. I felt like we were in a Scooby Doo episode. We ran around the house to the front yard where the trip wire was set up. We hopped over the wire, leading the creature into the trap. He tripped the wire and the cage came down; he was caught.

The creature was not too happy with his new home. He started jumping up and down, shaking the cage, and even tried to bite through the metal. We called the police and told them what we caught. We heard the sirens in the distance and spotted about twenty-five police cars pulling into the neighborhood. The chief asked how we caught the creature, and I told him. He was shocked that a bunch of teenage kids could catch a giant creature like this. As we opened the cage to get a closer look at the creature, the chief noted something wrong. He grabbed the back of the monster's neck and pulled down a zipper. The chief drew his weapon as a tiny man stepped out of the costume. The tiny man hit a button on the suit he was wearing and blasted off into the sky. We all were amazed and really didn't understand what had just happened. I said, "So you guys want to go get some breakfast?" The police officers agreed, and we were on our way. I guess this mystery will just have to go unsolved.

Visiting Hours

I lost the most important and meaningful person in my life. My grandma passed away from a brain tumor when I was young. The date was June 27, 2004. I often hear people say that time heals all wounds and that someday the pain will subside, but I can tell you they lied. It has been ten years and I still feel pain from her death. The pain, however, did ease last summer vacation. A day I could never forget, when God came down and granted me visiting hours with my grandma.

In the summer, I always cut the rose brushes and repainted the statue of the Virgin Mary my family had outside our home. My grandma loved roses, and had strong Catholic roots, so I kept a rose garden and the statue out front in her memory. The sunset that night was like I had never seen before. I watched with an unwavering gaze as a fiery red orb of light slowly sank beneath the horizon and threads of light lingered in the sky, mingling with the rolling clouds, dyeing the heavens first orange, then red, then dark blue, until all that was left of the sunset was a chalky mauve. Then a beam of bright light suddenly came from the sky. I heard beautiful singing and trumpets playing from the sky. I stood in utter amazement as the light beams that burst from the sky turned into a golden walkway.

A gentle, but mighty voice emerged saying, "Come up my child. Your visiting hours are running."

I stepped up on the golden walkway, grabbed the golden hand rails, and began to walk up into the sky. The singing became more beautiful as I continued getting closer to the end. The stairs stopped at an old wooden door with a bronze door knob. The door was not attached to anything; it was like the door was hovering in the air afraid to touch the cloud.

"Well hello there! You must be Posey's grandson Joey," said a beautiful woman sitting at a desk.

The woman had auburn hair that curled naturally at the ends and reached below her shoulder blades. Her skin was between the color porcelain and light beige, not too light. Her almond shaped eyes were a hazel color. Her body type was slender and feminine.

She had beautiful, full eyebrows that framed her face, a few freckles that played across her nose and cheeks. She had a smile that was kind and genuine. She had a touch of makeup on that brought out her pink, full lips and rosy cheeks and she was wearing a modest, but cute white dress. Her demeanor was confident and sweet. She looked like an angel, but had no wings.

"Yes, ma'am I am him", I said in response.

She arose from the chair, came back from around the desk, grabbed my hand, and said, "you know it's rude to leave your grandmother waiting don't you? Poor Posey has been waiting since 2004 for your arrival. She is in the rose garden right now reading, I believe. She uses roses for bookmarks and knows nobody will take them from her book. Keep up child, right this way."

I wondered how this woman knew that when I was younger I used to pull my grandma's bookmark out of her books so she would not remember where her spot was. I shook that thought from my mind and tried to keep up with the woman, while trying to take in the sights and people that were around me. There were children playing and interacting with each other from every nation: North America, South America, Europe, Africa, and Asia. It was a miracle how each child spoke a different language, but they could understand each other. They were all dressed in the clothing style of their home country. I noticed a boy with a deerskin loincloth. He was barefoot, wore feathers from a turkey fashioned into a head dress, and had red paint down his broad tan chest. I noticed a Viking boy with a heavy fur coat and a horned helmet. A sweet little girl caught my eye as I continued on, she was about five years old. She wore a dress with a stiff light blue bodice that fastened at the back with a separate white full skirt. Gold strings were attached to the bodice shoulders. A pink linen chemise, worn underneath, peeked out just below the hem of her skirt. Another young boy appeared to be from an ancient period. He wore a tunic down to his knees. It was white with a crimson border. The girl playing with him wore a simple white tunic with a gold belt at the waist. Her long golden-red hair was held up by a jeweled hairpin, and a silver Bulla hung from her neck. The Bulla contained an amulet. Romans believed the Bulla would protect them from evil. As we continued walking, another young boy caught my eye. I stopped in my tracks and admired the young African boy. He wore a pure white oversized linen shirt that touched his knees. The linen shirt had long rips in the back, exposing his bare back. His back was lined with ridged scars that went every direction. He turned around and smiled a toothy grin at me. His dark hair was cut short and his green eyes looked right back at me. His eyes told a clear story of hurt, despair, and loneliness. He tried to hide behind the toothy smile and forget about the pain, but couldn't. His hands and feet had old hand-made shackles wrapped around them. Funny how the force driving the metal to form those shackles was the same force that induced the ridged scars across his back. The human touch is a bittersweet sense.

"That is Henry. What a special child he is," Izzy said.

"Why does he still have those heavy chains on his wrists and ankles? And those scars on his back?" I asked.

Izzy looked at him once more and said, "We offered to take them off and remove the scars from his back when he arrived, but he said no. He wanted to keep them on as a constant reminder of how hard it was to gain freedom, and the physical, emotional, and spiritual hurt he went through. He said Jesus still has his battle wounds, so why should I get rid of mine?"

Henry was six, but his outlook on life was remarkable. Keeping the wounds on his body and the chains around his hands and ankles serves to remind people freedom is a tough road to achieve. We walked a little farther and a beep came from Izzy's wrist.

"Well Joey, I must go. Someone is waiting for me at the gate. I'll call Kristen and she will take you the rest of the way. She will be right over," she said departing from me.

I sat down on the bench and continued my people watching. I saw two girls wearing kalasiris with shawls over them, playing with dolls. Next to them were another pair of girls who wore gowns that came down to the ankles, with a high round collar and tight sleeves to the wrist. The fringe and cuffs were decorated with embroidery and a band was wrapped around the upper arm. White, gold, and silver clothing were a common theme. All the children were doing different activities with each other. Some were passing a ball made from leather skin filled with chaff, dry papyrus reeds tied tightly together with strings. Others were playing the hoop and pole game. Calculi boards were set up and children faced each other seeing who could win the most consecutive games. Some children were coloring, drawing, writing, and conversing with one another. What an amazing sight to see all the children from all different time periods and parts of the world coming together and getting along.

"Joey?" a lovely voice rang out.

"Yes ma'am. I am him." I answered.

"Oh, heavens! You can call me Kristen. None of this ma'am stuff. You're making feel old, " she said.

"If you insist miss," I replied.

"Come this way. We don't have much time now," she said.

Kristen was wearing a long white dress with a gold belt wrapped around her waist. The lustrous, pearl-beaded fabric of her dress glinted in the light. It fit her flawlessly. The dress molded her torso beautifully, complimenting her feminine shape. The dress draped past her toes, slightly drifting from her legs as she walked. She was about 5'4" tall. She was elegant with a strong bone structure; bread could be sliced on her cheekbones. Her eyes were an icy blue color, a blue I have never seen before. Her face had a sharp alertness to it, and her nose was small and wrinkled up tightly when she laughed, a small flaw that makes her look like a real person who you could talk to and know, rather than an airbrushed model. Her skin was smooth and even when she was still. When concentrating on something, the ghost of a smile touched her lips. She had visible angel wings which were closed together as she walked. We walked for a lengthy period of time. The sun was still shining, the cloudless blue sky sat above, and angels were still playing and singing, but there was a Jazzy tune playing further in the distance. I ran ahead of Kristen following the crisp jazz tune that pleased my ear drums. The smooth vibrations of the drumstick striking the trap was quivering just above the cool raspy slide of the steel brush caressing the snare. The sound of saxophones lowly moans; its melody so pure rings in my ears. I can feel the thrum of the bass like a slow pulse coursing through my body. Blood beats through my veins in rhythm with the drums. The saxophone keens a wordless melody like a barren maternal heart. Every note that pours from the singer's throat is a full and clear audible soul. The piano's harmony dances almost visibly around my head and chest, pulsing with each thump of the bass.

"You might recognize these people up the road. We will sit and listen for a while," Kristen said.

Music was my life and my grandma always wanted me to pick up the piano, so I did, and picked up the bass guitar along the way. The jazz music was soothing to the ear and every note was hit with perfect precision. We arrived at a massive lounge resembling a jazz bar. There were people sitting at round tables conversing, a barkeep serving drinks, people making toasts, and smoking cigars. Five men were playing on a dimly lit stage. We took a seat at a table right in front of the stage. The pianist wore a blue tux with blue pants to match. He had on a white shirt with black studs for buttons and black cuff links. His hands shook back and forth rapidly over the keys. His body swayed with the music, and round brown glasses with black lens covered his eyes.

"He can play that piano, can't he Jack?" Kristen said.

"He sure can. My name is Joey, not Jack," I responded. "I know. Do you know who that is?" she asked. "Well, that's Ray. No one can play that piano better than he can," I said with a grin.

The other four men looked familiar as well. The bassist was old Jimmy Blanton, the inventor of the bass solo. The drummer was Tommy Benford; sax was occupied by Johnny Hodges, and the singer was Louis Armstrong. The band played Ray's famous song, "What I'd Say", my favorite arrangement of his. Kristen took me by the hand and led me out the door. We continued walking down the golden path.

"See the girl with the red dress on? She can do the birdland all night long. Yeah yeah, what I'd say, all right," Ray sang out.

I mumbled the words to the next verse as the music began to fade out as Izzy and I walked further down the golden path. In the distance I saw a blue-green ivory doorway with bright green grape vines weaving through its bars. The golden path we were walking on turned into a smooth stone pathway. A beautiful landscape greeted us on the other side of the gate. It was wide and open, sloping gently down to a cosmic-blue river. A grove of cypress pines flanked us on one side, while a thick grove of peaceful beeches stood guard on the other. Apple trees ran through the center of the garden, casting a lake of claw shadows onto the grass. The blackbird was the main player in the dawn chorus, his song as clear and fresh as the garden he will later raid. Warbling wrens and caroling chaffinches joined him, creating an orchestra of sound. It cascaded into the open spaces, like ghosts through windows, and onto the smiling lips of the sleepers within. This earthy song of nature roused the rest of the animals from their slumber. Dozy hedgehogs tottered like zombies as they got drunk on the last of the rotten apples. Butterflies fluttered through the air with their velvet wings. As the grass in the garden grew to Jurassic heights, pheasants clucked like cockerels and sprinted like roadrunners, celebrating our arrival. An old oak patio sat in the middle of the garden. On the patio was a white bench suspended in the air. A woman dressed in a pearl white dress occupied it. She was swinging back and forth, reading, and humming. At her feet sat dozens and dozens of roses, all having different colored petals. Some were the traditional red, others were colors I had never seen in a rose before.

"Grandma?" I asked.

She looked up from her book and her brown colored eyes met mine for the first time in ten years. She placed the book down at her side, rose up from her chair, and hugged me tight. The hug was magical. Tears trickled down my face, the animal's song muted, and I felt secure. The hug was soft, gentle, and comforting.

"Joey, I have missed you so much," she said still hugging me tight.

"Why did you have to leave me Grandma? Why couldn't you talk to me? Why?" I cried out.

"Come sit down with me for a while. I'll do the best I can to answer your questions. I gave you signs throughout this trip that show you I have been watching out for you," she said smiling.

"You have?" I asked.

"The first sign was when God called you up here for a visit. Izzy was at the front desk to greet you. Your favorite eye color on a woman is hazel and you find it cute when they have freckles across their nose," Grandma said.

I smiled, knowing she was correct. I listened as she continued.

"I know you enjoy music and beautiful women. I sent Kristen here to bring you to me. I know your love for Jazz music, so I sent Ray and the boys to play your favorite tune. I knew the pain and suffering you went through freshman year in high school, and I know how much you enjoy the presence of little kids. I had Izzy show you all the children of different nationalities. Most importantly, I had her show you Henry."

"Why? What does Henry have to do with my freshman year?" I rudely interrupted.

"Henry is a fighter. He is a strong willed young boy. His faith in God is powerful. He respects where he came from and who he is. Just like you, Joey. You are a fighter. When things went wrong and you were at your lowest point, you did not give up or give in. You turned to God and let him lead you out of darkness and into a new light. You put your trust in God. You made an awful experience into a positive one. You still show your scars by writing and telling others what happened to you. Henry still has his scars as well. His are visible, however; yours are invisible and marked on your heart. Kristen brought you here to me for a purpose as well. I know how you enjoy women who dress modestly, and have blue eyes. I had Kristen take you through the garden because I know how much you love to be out in nature. When I watch you out on the golf course, sometimes, I call Michelangelo to paint a stunning sunset for you. That is why golf is the perfect sport for you. The golf courses you play on each have something special about them. Every golf course is different and you are constantly surrounded by nature. With baseball you could not see that. You didn't get the opportunity to spend time in nature to see the trees bloom, the flowers blossom, and the sun set," she said.

We sat there for what felt like hours taking in all the beauty of nature around us.

"My son, you're visiting hours are up. It is time to go back now," said a mighty voice.

"It's time Joey. God is taking you back now. Remember the sunshine always comes after the rain, and I am always watching over you," Grandma said in my ear while we exchanged hugs.

"Oh, God leave me here. Please! I am not ready to leave," I cried.

Kristen grabbed my hand tightly and said, "An angel is what she was meant to be. I know it's hard to see. She is watching over her family and you night and day. Saying I love you in her own special way. In the night you sleep and in the day you miss her but she watches you all from her star in the sky. So remember, when you're on the roof at night, look to the sky and send her a smile".

Kristen picked me up and brought me back to earth. We hugged goodbye and I proceeded back inside my house. It was late, about eleven or so. My mother, grandpa, and Aunt Barb were all asleep. I quietly walked upstairs using my iPhone flashlight to guide me. I tip-toed around Barb's room, unlocked the window, took the screen out and carefully sat it down. I slid out the window, quiet as a mouse. I grabbed my bass guitar and sat in my usual get-a-way spot. The night was cool, the sky was clear, and there was a plethora of stars in the sky. I remembered what Kristen had told me about looking for the brightest star in the sky. I played a blues song on my bass thinking to myself, there is no way I will find grandma in all these stars. As I finished up playing the blues I looked up to the sky one last time hoping to see grandma. Out of the black sky a bright shooting star shot through the sky. The star gave off so much light it was like daytime. The star vanished as quickly as it started. I looked up to the sky, smiled and said, "Thank you Grandma. I knew you wouldn't let me down. You have never let me down before why would I think this time would be any different/ I love you to the moon and back, remember that".

Section 3: Personal Essay & Memoir

Life, Love, Loss

Chapter One
Froshie

Froshie year wasn't the best year for me. Bullying took place, names were thrown at me, and death threats were posed. I did everything in my power to bring justice to this situation. I called witnesses, showed proof, and named the names of the kids that were calling me a Nigger or an uneducated nigger, but nothing worked. I came home and found a little posted note that said, "Never forget who you are or where you came from, love Mr. Tindal." I took that saying to heart and decided that each day every time someone would post a death threat or call me a nasty name I would write a line of a poem about who I was and where I came from. Writing a line each day would help me remember how I got to where I was. I finished the poem at the end of freshman year when I thought all the bullying and bull was over. The poem read:

Where I'm From

I am from a family

from members whose love is as big as the universe

I am from grass and dirt

from home plate, white lines, and people in masks

I am from lines on a court

from a ten foot high basket and an orange ball

I am from numbers like math

from sand and one hundred meters

I am from green grass

from clubs, carts, and caddies

I am from a school where there is NO COLOR

from a princiPAL who ONLY sees WHITE and not **BLACK**

I am from a neighborhood

from friends with works bomb, bonfires, and fireworks

I am from Hocus Pocus Joey on Locust

performing tricks like an acrobat

I am from sounds sweet as ripe berries

from keyboards, strings and brass

I am from Destiny's Step Child

from playing bass to the sounds of rock and blues

I am from church

from catholic teaching

I am from St Roch CYO a tether to my roots

from laser, putt putt, and service projects

I am from the Wizards guard

from Dorothy, scarecrow, lion, tin man, and Toto.

Chapter Two

Gifts

I let go of the things that unfolded during Froshie year and was ready to start a new chapter in Joey Roembke's life. I found another note at the beginning of sophomore year from my best friend, Jack Madden. The note read, "Hey Prince I thought you needed some cheering up after what bull came about last year and found something you might like. I was looking up quotes and pictures that I could draw to cheer you up and came across the word H.O.P.E but each letter stood for a different word and these made a phrase. (H)old (O)n (P)ain (E)nds. Remember if you hold on the pain will end bro and just remember you have been given gifts by God. God knew you would find a way to make something positive out of a negative situation. I love you Bro; see you around. Love, Jack". Jack's note spoke to my heart, and he was right I was given gifts from God. I just had to figure what they were and how I could use them. I wrote another poem line by line just like the one I wrote freshman year. I wrote a line every time I thought I noticed a gift from God or a message from God. The poem took weeks to finish.

My Gifts

What gifts I bring you ask

Now I look upon my past

Once an athlete thought I

Whether basketball, golf, or track, I run, I fly

I wondered is it music I bring

The sounds of instruments I love but do not sing

It is friendships I share

On Twitter, Facebook, and everywhere

It is family, we're so close

They support me the most

I now know it isn't any of these

But an opportunity I must seize

It is diversity I brought that has had the most impact

Shedding the light on education we lack

A different person one broken hearted

Changed forever from when I started

Now stronger, wiser, put to the test

To stand up for others I'll do my best

Cause who I am matters ya know

Afro-American Sophomore Joe

Chapter 3

A Lost Life

Junior year arrived quickly and I was ready for the new school year. Junior year started smooth. No worries, no ignorance or stupidity going on, just smooth sailing. My grades were up the highest they have ever been. I was enjoying my classes and my teachers were great, but this smooth sailing wouldn't stay smooth for very long. Around 10:30 on a November night, I received a call on my cell from Jack. Jack sounded down and I asked what's going on? Jack told me our friend, Kyle, committed suicide earlier that night. The silence between Jack and I was so quiet you could hear a piece of pencil lead drop. I said to Jack we will get through this. We have lost a close friend, but we will push on I promise. Jack said, I know we will. Just go write a poem bro and you'll be good. I did what Jack told me to and wrote this poem on my phone.

A Lost Life

I jumped, you caught me.

I laughed, you joked.

I was down, you picked me up.

I crumbled, you glued me back together.

I loved you, you loved me back

You jumped, I couldn't catch you

You forgot to laugh, I couldn't remind you.

You were down, I couldn't hold you.

You crumbled, I had no glue.

You loved me, I still love you.

Without a warning or sign you ventured to a world divine.

I refused to say goodbye.

Yet tonight I cry my tears are for you my friend, but our legacy will not end.

I will see you soon, but first I have living to do.

I promise I won't forget.

Your face is embedded in my heart.

Chapter 4

Love Huh?

The next day was awful for the Roncalli community. The passing periods were silent, hugs given back and forth between friends, and tears running from everyone's eyes. The school continued on with the regular plans to have liturgy. The liturgy was hard to get through, but friends were picking up friends and everyone pushed through it. At the end of the liturgy, however, Mr. Weisenbach made a remark that pulled the heart strings and snapped them. He said the three most powerful, meaningful, and most important words "I Love You". I went home that day and once again put the pencil to the paper and wrote a poem which really isn't a poem more of rant.

Love Huh?

Love is not self-centered.

Love is not blind.

Love is not just words.

Love is actions.

Love is a back bone.

Love is there when you need it the most.

You said you "Loved" me.

How come when I came to you when I was being harassed, picked on, called hateful names, given death threats, and feeling like life was hopeless you turned your back on me?

How come when I gave you the names of the people who were doing these things nothing was done? How come when I showed the letter that had the threats on them you continued to do nothing? How come when I brought you witnesses, and they told you what they called me, you just said it wasn't mean spirited and they did not mean anything by it? I know why. You, the person who just said you "loved" me wanted to protect YOURSELF and the reputation of your precious school. You swept everything under the rug and turned a blind eye to a major flaw in your school. You said all the right words such as "I'll take care of it" but you didn't take action and back them up.

I needed you, I trusted you, I believed in you.

I thought I could rely on you to fix the problem, to help someone out and support them.

I thought you were my PrinciPAL.

I needed a back bone because the one I had was struck so many times it fell apart.

I needed you to be that back bone.

I needed a friend to lean on.

You weren't there for me.

You turned your back on me when I needed you most.

Now you expect me to believe that YOU "love" me?

You don't even know what love is.

Love is too complex for your perfect mind set

You didn't show me love then. What makes you think I believe for one second that you are going to show me it now?

I don't believe you, trust you, or rely on you anymore.

I was a fool for believing that you "loved" me in the first place.

You need to get out of the imaginary world you are in and snap back into reality.

You need to realize that real problems are happening in YOUR school.

You don't love me and never will, so stop feeding me this bullshit about how you "Love" me when me and you both know it's not true.

It was a hell of a try though.

It was believable with the tears and all, but you're not fooling me this time…

The Difference

I constantly hear students complain about school. Saying how much they hate it, calling it dumb and stupid, and say there is no point in even going. They complain also about the number of tests they have in a week, the teachers, the load of homework, the rules, how early they have to wake up, and how pointless they think an assignment is. I always dread school, but school only. I love to learn new things, but I do not love school. There is a significant difference between learning and school; people tend to overlook it. The difference is simple, but we tend to ignore the simplest of answers. First is school, followed by learning.

School is indeed waking up early and going to a place full of people who judge you, whom act a certain way when they are with you, but different when you are not around. School is when you're told to be yourself, but people judge you for who you are. People who gossip, make up lies, and start rumors without knowing if it is true. School is having short, useless information shoved down your throat. Information that is only needed to be retained for a short period of time, then gets thrown out after a test or quiz. School is where you spend all your time in a classroom "listening" to a teacher going on and on about a certain subject you may or may not care about. School is being judged on how well you remember the information the teachers give you. School is where you are judged by a long slip of paper, numbered one through fifty, with five answers to choose from "a" through "e". School is where most of your stress comes from; studying material for a test until late hours into the night, trying to get involved in numerous activities around school, trying to please your parents by keeping your grades up, trying to figure what to do after high school, what college to go to, and what area of study to major in. All these things are difficult to balance and obtain when eight hours is spent in a building where all people do is judge. That is what school is all about in a nutshell.

Learning, however, is a million times better than school. You are probably asking yourself the question "Don't we go to school to learn things"? Yes, everyone goes to school to learn the different subject areas, but learning is different than just knowing how to use the Pythagorean Theorem, or being able to recite all of the fifty state capitals. Learning is going to places where you have never been before. Learning is making multiple mistakes throughout life, but learning from each and every one of them. Learning is gaining a lesson out of the mistakes to help better yourself. Learning is discovering new things you never knew before--discovering what is enjoyable, what is not pleasing, and finding out who you are. Learning is finding out what it takes to be successful. Learning is knowing what questions to ask. Learning is getting out of your comfort zone, discovering new talents and hobbies not noticed before. Learning is taking existing knowledge and modifying it, refining it, and changing it for the better. Learning is building upon what is already known. Learning cannot all happen at once. Learning is a process, rather than a collection of factual information. Learning is gaining more knowledge to better understand the complex world around you. Without learning, you would be lost in the world you live in. See the difference?

Grandma

History books are filled with the names and biographies of influential individuals, thereby impressing everyone with their importance. These same people sometimes even have movies produced or books written about them. However, the important person who influenced me has not the same notoriety -- no books, no movies, no famous name. Throughout my life, one person's influence left a lasting mark on the most special part of the human body, my heart. My grandma planted an everlasting seed in my heart that is an important part of who I am today.

She went by Posey. Although her birth name was Rosemary, everyone called her Posey. She was the definition of perfection to me. She stood only about five feet two inches tall, her stunning brown eyes complemented her beautiful face, hair as white as a fresh snowfall --perfectly done every day -- she always dressed to impress. The attribute I admire most was her unconditional love she gave to everyone she met. My grandma's love for me remains a part of who I am and everything I do.

For many years, I pursued the game of baseball. As I matured, I began to notice how easy the game came to me and thought I would be playing baseball for the rest of my days. My grandma was my biggest and most dedicated fan when I was little. She came to every game whether near or far, just to watch me play. Her tan flower-covered chair stood in place on the left field line every game. I can still hear her shouting advice from the outfield and remember how I listened, doing exactly what she told me. I valued her opinion more than anyone else because she knew me the best.

In 2004, my grandma became seriously ill. The illness took a noticeable toll on her both physically and mentally. The once flawless face became marked with large black splotches, the beautiful eyes that gleamed brightly became shadowed by darkness, and her white hair turned a yellowed stale gray. She could not attend my games anymore; she could not eat on her own; and, the loving words she used to speak were hushed by the illness. She fought sickness with all she had, but the illness was too powerful and unforgiving. My grandma passed later that year.

The days following her death were unbearable. I felt like a nail was being pounded in my heart repeatedly. I lost my biggest fan, my greatest role model, and my best friend. My grandma had talked to my mom about me as I played my baseball games, telling my mother something that would change my life for the better. I was twelve at the time and remember asking my mom what grandma and she talked about at my games years ago.

My mom said, "sit down Joey and I'll tell you." I took a seat, afraid what my mom might say. She took a deep breath and continued, "Your grandma never really wanted you to play baseball. It's not what she had pictured you doing. She pictured you playing golf instead of baseball."

I recalled my grandma always said to me, "Joey, you can play any sport you want to play, but make sure you're not playing because you just like the sport. Play it because you love it. Be passionate about your choice." I took these words to heart and followed them.

After a freshman year playing baseball, I decided to try the game of golf. I went out for the golf team my sophomore year and have played on the team for three years. I sometimes miss playing between the white lines but I knew the seed my grandma planted would not grow if I did not at least try playing golf. Every day, I devote myself to the practice and play of golf. The more I play, the better I am at golf, the more food I give to the seed that allows my talent to bloom.

It is crazy to think about, is it not? That one person can change a life, a direction, and a future without the person even being here. My grandma knew me and knew what I loved more than anything. My grandma told my mother about golf for a reason. She knew that golf was what I loved from the beginning…not baseball, but golf. My grandma taught me an everlasting lesson which impacts my future choices. The lesson is that I have to do what I love. She taught me that just because I am good at a sport and it comes easily to me does not mean it is the right event for me. I have to love it, want to play it every day, and push to improve upon my skills every day. As a result, I have decided to study Professional Golf Management at Eastern Kentucky University. In my heart, I know this is the right choice. Like the seed planted in my heart, my love for the game grows every day.

Forever Changed

Life happens, and we are changed forever. I am not the same person I was before attending Roncalli. Now I see life from a different perspective. Throughout grade school, people told me the high school years would be the greatest of my life. I looked forward to attending Roncalli; the desire to be accepted and to be a Roncalli Rebel was all I wanted. However, the first day of school would be the last day I would walk through the doors of Roncalli believing that just being me was enough.

In high school, I planned to be a Rebel, go to class, and play sports. The fact I was one of only a handful of African-American students in the entire school did not concern me until the second day of school. That was the first time someone told an obnoxious, racial joke during lunch. I did not know how to respond, so I laughed, but inside I was hurting. The racial jokes and slurs continued, and I wanted to transfer to a school where there were more minority students. I told my mom about the comments being made. She told me to consider the ignorance of the people making them and to walk away.

I tried to overlook it and walk away, but inside it was painful. A program called Rachel's Challenge, which addressed racism and the importance of judging people based on character versus outward appearances, was presented to the student body. I thought this might help my situation. I was wrong again. Shortly after this program, I became a target for racial slurs and threats, especially in the junior hallways between classes. I was called a "nigger" and a "coon" as I passed by upperclassmen. I had no idea the meaning of a coon or lynching. I was told I was an "uneducated nigger and the scum of the earth" by students I knew and some I did not. I ignored them, but each time I felt a piece of me disappearing or at least the "Joey" I always thought to be me. As I was opening my locker one day, I found a piece of paper sticking out of it. I proceeded to open it, and it had one word on it, "nigger". I crumpled the note and threw it away.

Unfortunately, the harassing continued. We were just beginning to read "To Kill a Mocking Bird", and my mom asked if I knew the subject of the book. I told her "yes". Then, I told her the situation at school had escalated and she was appalled. I was ashamed to tell her what people had been calling me because I thought the problem was me. I was hurt by what was being said. I felt lonely and depressed. I just wanted to be a Rebel. I continued to receive notes in my locker. One note said, "Get out. Call the KKK on you. We lynch you. Nigger. Die Nigger", so I decided to show this note to the Dean of Students. My friends, who were with me when I found the note, went with me. The Dean indicated he would look into the matter and also tell the Principal. He said there was not much he could do if we did not know who was responsible.

At this point, I just felt like the whole world turned against me. My mom, uncles, and I went to school to meet with the Dean, the President, and the Resource teacher. I was afraid of possible reprisal, but I wanted the comments and notes to stop. I provided names of students I knew; I looked at my cousin's yearbook and identified others. Because I felt threatened, I was escorted to class by football players, and the contents of my locker were moved. I took different hallways and stairs to avoid being harassed. The basketball and baseball coaches were supportive and talked to three of the student athletes who had been part of the problem. The coaches required the athletes to apologize to my mom and me for their comments. The Principal spoke to all Channel 1 classes about bullying and inappropriate, insensitive comments. After hearing these talks, I thought maybe the depressing days were finally over.

However, the notes continued and the darkness seemed to consume me. What was wrong with me? Why could I not fit in? Each note seemed to be worse than the previous. One note said, "You have three days to get out or (a noose was drawn on the paper)". Christmas was coming, and I did not even care. In spite of the three apology letters written by the student athletes, the school's investigation could not find a single person who admitted anything said was "mean spirited". Not a single student received even a detention for their actions. Not a single parent was called. I had to decide what I wanted to do. Did I want to stay at Roncalli? Would I fit in better somewhere else?

I chose to stay at Roncalli because running was not the answer. I did nothing wrong. I had a right to be at Roncalli. I took solace in the support my family provided from beginning to end. They were there for me when I was hurting and struggling just to go to school. My teachers and coaches were supportive. I know racism is not just about the Underground Railroad, Martin Luther King, and slavery. Experiencing racism feels so different than reading about it.

I wrote a letter to the Roncalli School Board asking they not turn a blind eye or sweep these acts under a rug but to change how they address these situations in the future. I asked the Board to "see if you could have walked in my shoes without taking them off."

Yes, I have changed. Life happens, and we are forever changed. I will never be the same person I was on the first day at Roncalli. Before all this racism unfolded, I did not really see color. It was like I was living life through a black and white television not noticing the differences in people's appearance. However, the channel has changed, and I no longer see in black and white but in different shades of color. Try as I might, I cannot get it to go back. I am truly forever changed by what occurred.

The Seed

"Heaven plants a special seed, and we must have faith for these. Red, yellow, black, and white they are precious in the Father's eyes." Amy Grant is right, I am a special seed. I was adopted as a newborn. My family has watered the seed and given me love, care, and a safe home. Until freshman year came along, I did not think much about being adopted. That year the sprouting seed was stepped on and nearly ruined by the ignorance of narrow-minded people. "All you'll ever be is a faded memory of a bully." The lyrics in the song, "Bully" by Shinedown made me realize that I have to let go of the past. People who bully are forever just being bullies, nothing more nothing less. Junior year the seed popped through, bloomed and life at last was good. "Loving living it's all good" by Will Smith is my motto going through my days now. While life is not easy, music provided inspiration and helped me through the hard times.

"Every life, every beating heart has a searching soul inside ever needing, ever seeking out the meaning of life." These lyrics by Amy Grant paint a beautiful picture and message about a child who's adopted. My mother listened to this song and thought of me when she was ready to adopt. Growing up, I really didn't know what being different meant or even what adoption was. I always knew I was adopted and I knew about being biracial. My mom told me one day to listen to "Children of the World" by Amy Grant and the song lyrics hit home. The song is not only about adoption, but the right to life. My birth mom was only nineteen years old when she had me. My birth mother gave me life and out of love, gave me up for adoption three days after I was born. She knew she could not give me the life she wanted me to have. She chose my mom because she knew my mom would love me, care for me, and raise me right. My birth mother loved me enough, cherished life enough to give me to a family who would love me, and give me everything I needed. The seed was watered and tended and grew a little each day. I listen to the song once in a while because it helps me realize how precious life is. I am forever grateful my birth mother chose life and gave me up for adoption. I love my birth mother, mom, and my family. I hope one day I can meet by birth mother to thank her for giving me the precious gift of life. I am also anxious to see what she looks like and if I resemble her. There is a piece of me missing. The only way to fill that void is to meet the woman who gave birth to me. When I meet her, I truly hope it will help me to know who I am. Freshman year made me want to change who I was.

"Don't be unhappy, can't remember when I last saw you laughing. If this world makes you crazy and you've taken all you can bear. You call me up because you know I'll be there."   Freshman year, the world did give me all I could take, but Mr. Weisenbach was not there for me. The seed that was just budding was bruised and crushed by racist remarks and taunts. Mr. Weisenbach gave a speech this year about how he loved us and about how he would be there for us when we needed him. Freshman year was when I needed him the most, but he was nowhere to be found. Where was he when I was being bullied? Why did he not take action to stop it? Why did he not punish the people who called me the "Nigger" or used demeaning racial slurs? He expects me to believe that he loves me. Actions speak louder than words. The racist comments escalated as the days went on. Threatening notes appeared in my locker during the day. One note said, "Get out. Call the KKK on you. We lynch you. Nigger. Die Nigger". My locker had to be moved; I took different routes to my classes escorted by football players. I could not take it anymore and had thought of giving up. My mom, my family, and my resource teachers were there every step of the way for me. They helped me through the hardest and most depressing time of my life. That's a true example of love. The song "True Colors" by artist Cyndi Lauper says, "I see your true colors and that's why I love you. So don't be afraid to let them show. Your true colors," had a significant meaning in my life. "True colors are beautiful, like a rainbow," talks about the beauty of being true to who you are. Freshman year I was afraid of being me. My mom, uncles, and I had meetings with the administration and sent letters to the school board to get to the bottom of this issue. The meetings were no use and the administration swept everything under the rug, pretending that this never happened to me, when in reality, it did. This changed my life forever, my grades suffered; my participation in sports was negatively impacted. I just thought if I was different these events would not be happening. No action, no punishment, no nothing was done to the kids who bullied me. It just said to me that I was not worthy as a person. That is what bothered me the most. The ultimate demonstration of racism is the failure to act or turning one's head when faced with racial bullying. I considered going to another school, but I knew I had done nothing wrong. I decided I was staying in spite of the way I had been treated by some of the kids and the school administration. I did not really see color. It was like I was living life through a black and white television not noticing the differences in people's appearance. However, the channel has changed, and I no longer see in black and white but in different shades of color. My perception changed. I am truly forever changed by what occurred. Thankfully my junior year has been great.

The last year and a half have been excellent. My grades went up, my golf game improved, and I was not afraid of being who I was anymore. However early in my junior year one major down fall occurred and I still deal with it today. My close friend Kyle Baker took his own life. I was shocked, saddened, speechless, and dumbfounded as to why he did it. Kyle seemed fine at school talking to me, catching up on what happened that weekend. He appeared to be fine, and then he took his own life. Kyle introduced me to a song "Rain" by one of my favorite artists, Will Smith. Ever since Kyle died, I often listen to this song; it keeps me in a positive frame of mind. The song itself is about loving life and living life to its fullest.

"The sunshine always comes out after the rain" was the line that tugged my heart strings the most. During my high school years, I have learned staying positive in spite of bad days is important. Realizing bad days will happen, but superior days will always follow. A seed cannot grow and bloom without two things, sunlight and rain. While a seed cannot thrive without sunlight and rain, neither can a human being grow and bloom without weathering a few down days outweighed by the excellent ones which follow.

A Lesson from a Christmas Bear

Christmastime was always a magical time of year for me. The beautifully decorated shopping malls, with toys everywhere I looked, always fascinated me. The houses filled with lights that glowed upon the glistening snow at night were a beautiful sight. Decorating the Christmas tree and falling asleep underneath the warm glow of the lights, in awe that Santa Claus would soon be there, was the best part of it all. As a child, these things enchanted me. Sure, the presents were great, but the excitement and mystery of Christmas was what I loved most of all. Believing…that is what it was all about. Believing there really was a Santa and waking up Christmas morning realizing Santa had come, as my sleepy eyes focused on all the fancily wrapped presents under the tree.

Christmas was a fun time to enjoy the company of my family. It all started on Christmas Eve day; I woke in the morning and prepared myself by helping clean up the house. It took a good two hours to cover the whole house. By the time the house was cleaned, it was time for my family to come over. The time I shared with my family was spent talking about old stories that had happened in our lives throughout the years.

Christmas morning arrived, and I jumped out of bed and ran downstairs screaming Santa; Santa was here! My mom and aunt awoke and walked downstairs to see what all Santa brought. My mom told me to open up a certain present that was from Santa. I ripped open the reindeer - designed wrapping paper and found a book inside titled, *Peef the Christmas Bear*. I really did not know what to think because I was not into reading. However, the story of Peef was interesting and not like the other Christmas stories I had heard; this one was unique. The story went something like this... Santa is up to something! He asked all of his elves to pick out their favorite fabric and bring it to him. Just what is Santa doing? Why was he making a multi-colored Christmas Bear? When the final stitch was completed and with a push from Santa's finger, the bear speaks his own name...Peef.

Peef was an important bear. He was Santa's chief assistant and dearly loved Santa. However, what Peef really wanted was to belong to and bring happiness to a special child. That does not seem to be Peef's fate until one Christmas Eve when Santa was one toy short. Peef's dream was realized as he was left behind to bring one child great happiness. That special child was me.

After I was done reading the book, my mom brought me another box, which was bigger than the first one. I was really hyped because it was big and had a large blue bow on it. I quickly tore through the paper and was surprised to find Peef was lying inside the box. I jumped up and down in joy because I finally had a friend that could keep me company. Little did I know that later on Peef would teach me an important life lesson.

Peef was about two feet tall and constructed of many different colors. His feet were made of different material. The left foot was green and red plaid, and the right foot was white with red polka dots with "Peef" stitched on it. The arms also had different patterns on them. The left had green with white polka dots and the right was purple with black, wavy lines. The nose, mouth, and belly button were stitched in black. The right ear had red and little white hearts on it, and the left ear was pink and had a plaid pattern. My favorite feature on Peef, though, was the belly button. When you pushed in on the belly button, he made a noise that sounded like Peef.

Being an only child, I had to be creative when it came to finding things to do around the house, but with my buddy Peef life was much more enjoyable. I took Peef everywhere… on planes, long road trips, and even on my Eighth grade trip to Washington D.C. Peef attracted all the ladies too, so why not bring him along? I could always rely on Peef for everything. I knew he would listen to me when I talked to him. I hugged him and slept with him and knew he would be there when I woke up. Peef was the best friend to me.

As many years passed and I grew older, Peef began to disappear from my life. When my room was redecorated, I stored Peef away in the attic. Life was going good and high school was rapidly approaching. As a freshman in high school, I really thought I would not need Peef. However, I realized at the beginning of freshman year I needed Peef more than ever.

My freshman year I was bullied for the color of my skin. I would put on a fake smile at home acting like everything was OK when in reality it was not. I went to my bedroom every day after school and found Peef. I told Peef everything just because I did not want to bother my mom with the ignorance that was occurring. I felt safe telling Peef because he was my best friend at the time, and since he was a bear, I knew he could not tell anyone.

Months went by and the bullying continued. I went to my room and updated Peef daily on the latest news. My mom, however, found out one day about the bullying when we were doing homework, and, she was not too happy. When all this was happening, I felt like Peef was there through it all. I knew that might sound crazy because he was just a bear, but he was more than just a bear to me. He was the greatest friend a kid could ever have had.

Peef taught me a lesson that I still remember. Although I knew he was not alive, could not talk, or show emotion, Peef really did teach me something important. Peef was formed of many different colors, patterns, and materials which made him unique from other stuffed bears. Peef was just like me; I was different from most everyone who attended Roncalli: Like Peef, I was made up of different colors too. Peef taught me that being different was not a reason to hide or be afraid. Being different was something that should be recognized, cherished, and respected. Being different was what makes me… me. It took many years to figure out what Peef was trying to teach me. He taught me to embrace my unique features and that being different was good.

My Dream

I have vivid dreams of what I want to become; some might say I am a dreamer. "Yesterday is history. Tomorrow is a mystery. And today? Today is a gift. That's why we call it the present," Babatunde Olatunji once said. I live in the present and want to tell you what it is like. When I look at what life was like for teenagers fifty years ago, I have found that many things have changed and some are the same. Whether it is today, fifty years ago, or fifty years from today, life as a teenager is very complicated, influenced by world events and personal experiences.

My life as a teenager is a challenge, but in a good way. Life is fantastic as a teenager in the year 2010. High school is going great and is an exciting experience. Graduating from elementary school to high school has been a far better experience than I thought it would be. I attend Roncalli High School and my classes are challenging. While high school is a big part of my life, I also have many other interests. I play bass guitar in a band, go to sporting events, play several sports, and enjoy being with my friends. Sometimes on the weekends we have a bonfire, eat s'mores, and enjoy each other's conversation. I like to listen to music on my iPod and text my friends on my cell phone. Life as a teenager in 2010 is frenetic; there is always a school function or sporting event to attend. I live with my family in a suburban neighborhood where fortunately crime is almost non-existent. My family has sacrificed to pay for me to attend a Catholic school where the academics are important but so is spiritual development. We learn each and every day, while at the same time we are privileged to also be able to pray openly. I consider myself fortunate to also have many good friends to spend time with. My life is influenced by the access I have to technology, media, family and school. It is also influence by what is happening all over the world.

The world today is very complex. The state of the economy is currently very fragile. Never before has the world seen such a slow economic recovery with so many people out of work and people who have lost their homes. My uncle lost his job over a year ago and has not found a new job. In addition to the economic crisis, our first African

American President was elected. He has had to deal with the worst oil spill in U.S. history which occurred in the Gulf of Mexico, a H1N1 pandemic influenza, and devastating wars in Iraq and Afghanistan. In 1960, President Kennedy was the youngest President elected, and most people were optimistic about life in the United States. He also had to deal with many world crises including the Cuban missile crisis and racial injustice. Television was just invented and was only monochrome with 3-4 channels available without remote control. However it was the beginning of world events playing out in our own homes. Just like our parents who grew up in the 60's we are impacted personally by remote events we watch unfold on the television and internet.

I enjoy watching sports on television, especially golf. One of my favorite athletes is professional golfer, Tiger Woods. He seemed to have it all, athletic prowess, on camera charisma, and a wife and children. It was recently reported that he divorced his wife. The divorce came after a story broke several months ago about Woods having multiple affairs. This is disheartening to me because he was my role model, my idol. I have grown up loving the game of golf and looking up to him. I still respect his athletic skill, but personally I do not have the same respect for him. Sports are such a big part of my life, and I have a dream of becoming a professional athlete or a coach. I want to be the kind of person teenagers will look up to. I look forward to the future and all it has to bring. I also hope that in 2060 there will be peace, including no wars, racial equality, and religious freedom. I hope that technology will be used to make the world a better place. In 2060, we can hope that the world's wealth and natural resources will be shared by all. I hope that President Obama in not the only African American President. I hope that when you are reading this, life is good for you too. Being a teenager is great, and I know I have a lot of fun with my friends. That's what I wish for you-- lots of friends and fun. I wish for you and your friends many opportunities and fulfilled dreams. The last fifty years have been very eventful and have shaped the lives of many teenagers.

Life as a teenager regardless of the year, decade, or century is influenced by world and personal events and as a result is complicated. Family and friends make a great deal of difference in how we see life and what choices we make. World events and technology influence how we utilize all we have. Real or not idols influence our hopes and dreams. Who we ultimately become is what matters. Whether it is today, fifty years ago, or fifty years from today, life as a teenager is very complicated, influenced by world events and personal experiences, it impacts who we become.

Raymond Joseph Roembke 2014

Joey Roembke is a freelance writer and poet. His fictional story *Lessons from the Past* and memoir *Forever Changed* were published in the 2014 Central and Southern Indiana Student Anthology by the Scholastic Art & Writing Awards. His latest project *Joey Roembke Heart and Soul,* includes Reflections and Poetry, Fiction, and Personal Essays & Memoirs. When Joey is not writing, he is on the golf course improving his game or spending time with family and friends.

www.ingramcontent.com/pod-product-compliance
Lightning Source LLC
Chambersburg PA
CBHW081157170626
46813CB00009B/3225